'This being a DeLillo novel, there are no
answers to the vast metaphysical dilemmas
of temporal existence. There are only the sort of
densely posited questions that take you to all sorts
of challenging places where you have forgotten
that fiction can actually take you'

The Times

'The handling is subtle and deft,
and it works powerfully'

Guardian

'Another formidable construction
by a very distinctive writer'

Evening Standard

'Of all [DeLillo's] post-*Underworld* novels,
Point Omega is the most interesting'

Sunday Times

'This elusive novel will grow in resonance
as the years pass, exposing an afflicted society
struggling to see the wood for the trees'

Time Out

POINT OMEGA

Don DeLillo, the author of fifteen novels, including
Point Omega, *Falling Man*, *White Noise* and *Libra*, has
won many honours in America and abroad, including the
National Book Award, the PEN/Faulkner Award for Fiction,
the Jerusalem Prize for his complete body of work and the
William Dean Howells Medal from the American Academy
of Arts and Letters for his novel *Underworld*. In 2010,
he received the PEN/Saul Bellow Award.
He has also written three plays.

NOVELS

Americana

End Zone

Great Jones Street

Ratner's Star

Players

Running Dog

The Names

White Noise

Libra

Mao II

Underworld

The Body Artist

Cosmopolis

Falling Man

SHORT STORIES

The Angel Esmeralda: Nine Stories

PLAYS

The Day Room

Valparaiso

Love-Lies-Bleeding

POINT OMEGA

A NOVEL

DON DELILLO

PICADOR

First published 2010 by Scribner, a division of Simon and Schuster, Inc., New York

First published in Great Britain 2010 by Picador

First published in paperback 2011 by Picador

This edition published 2012 by Picador
an imprint of Pan Macmillan, a division of Macmillan Publishers Limited
Pan Macmillan, 20 New Wharf Road, London N1 9RR
Basingstoke and Oxford
Associated companies throughout the world
www.panmacmillan.com

ISBN 978-1-4472-2439-6

1 3 5 7 9 8 6 4 2

A CIP catalogue record for this book is available from
the British Library.

Printed in the UK by CPI Group (UK) Ltd, Croydon, CR0 4YY

2006
LATE SUMMER /
EARLY FALL

Anonymity

There was a man standing against the north wall, barely visible. People entered in twos and threes and they stood in the dark and looked at the screen and then they left. Sometimes they hardly moved past the doorway, larger groups wandering in, tourists in a daze, and they looked and shifted their weight and then they left.

There were no seats in the gallery. The screen was free-standing, about ten by fourteen feet, not elevated, placed in the middle of the room. It was a translucent screen and some people, a few, remained long enough to drift to the other side. They stayed a moment longer and then they left.

The gallery was cold and lighted only by the faint gray shimmer on the screen. Back by the north wall the darkness was nearly complete and the man standing alone moved a hand toward his face, repeating, ever so slowly, the action of a figure on the screen. When the gallery door slid open and people entered, there was a glancing light from the area beyond, where others were gathered, at some distance, browsing the art books and postcards.

The film ran without dialogue or music, no soundtrack at all. The museum guard stood just inside the door and people leaving sometimes looked at him, seeking eye contact, some kind of understanding that might pass between them and make their bafflement valid. There were other galleries, entire floors, no point lingering in a secluded room in which whatever was happening took forever to happen.

The man at the wall watched the screen and then began to move along the adjacent wall to the other side of the screen so he could watch the same action in a flipped image. He watched Anthony Perkins reaching for a car door, using the right hand. He knew that

4

Anthony Perkins would use the right hand on this side of the screen and the left hand on the other side. He knew it but needed to see it and he moved through the darkness along the side wall and then edged away a few feet to watch Anthony Perkins on this side of the screen, the reverse side, Anthony Perkins using the left hand, the wrong hand, to reach for a car door and then open it.

But could he call the left hand the wrong hand? Because what made this side of the screen any less truthful than the other side?

The guard was joined by another guard and they spoke awhile quietly as the automatic door slid open and people came in, with kids, without, and the man went back to his place at the wall, where he stood motionless now, watching Anthony Perkins turn his head.

The slightest camera movement was a profound shift in space and time but the camera was not moving now. Anthony Perkins is turning his head. It was like whole numbers. The man could count the gradations in the movement of Anthony Perkins' head. Anthony Perkins turns his head in five incremental movements rather than one continuous motion. It was like bricks in a wall, clearly countable, not like the flight of an arrow or a bird. Then again it was not like or unlike anything. Anthony Perkins' head swiveling over time on his long thin neck.

It was only the closest watching that yielded this perception. He found himself undistracted for some minutes by the coming and going of others and he was able to look at the film with the degree of intensity that was required. The nature of the film permitted total concentration and also depended on it. The film's merciless pacing had no meaning without a corresponding watchfulness, the individual whose absolute alertness did not betray what was demanded. He stood and looked. In the time it took for Anthony Perkins to turn his head, there seemed to flow an array of ideas involving science and philosophy and nameless other things, or maybe he was seeing too much. But it was impossible to see too much. The less there was to see, the harder he looked, the more he saw. This was the point. To see what's here, finally to look

and to know you're looking, to feel time passing, to be alive to what is happening in the
smallest registers of motion.

Everybody remembers the killer's name,
Norman Bates, but nobody remembers the
victim's name. Anthony Perkins is Norman
Bates, Janet Leigh is Janet Leigh. The victim
is required to share the name of the actress
who plays her. It is Janet Leigh who enters the
remote motel owned by Norman Bates.

He'd been standing for more than three
hours, looking. This was the fifth straight day
he'd come here and it was the next-to-last day
before the installation shut down and went to
another city or was placed in obscure storage
somewhere.

No one entering seemed to know what to
expect and surely no one expected this.

The original movie had been slowed to a
running time of twenty-four hours. What he
was watching seemed pure film, pure time.
The broad horror of the old gothic movie was
subsumed in time. How long would he have
to stand here, how many weeks or months,
before the film's time scheme absorbed his

own, or had this already begun to happen? He approached the screen and stood about a foot away, seeing snatches and staticky fragments, flurries of trembling light. He walked around the screen several times. The gallery was empty now and he was able to stand at various angles and points of separation. He walked backwards looking, always, at the screen. He understood completely why the film was projected without sound. It had to be silent. It had to engage the individual at a depth beyond the usual assumptions, the things he supposes and presumes and takes for granted.

He went back to the wall at the north end, passing the guard at the door. The guard was here but did not count as a presence in the room. The guard was here to be unseen. This was his job. The guard faced the edge of the screen but was looking nowhere, looking at whatever museum guards look at when a room stands empty. The man at the wall was here but maybe the guard did not count him as a presence any more than the man counted the guard. The man had been here for days on end and for extended periods every day and anyway he was back at the wall, in the dark, motionless.

He watched the actor's eyes in slow transit across his bony sockets. Did he imagine himself seeing with the actor's eyes? Or did the actor's eyes seem to be searching him out?

He knew he would stay until the museum closed, two and a half hours from now, then come back in the morning. He watched two men enter, the older man using a cane and wearing a suit that looked traveled in, his long white hair braided at the nape, professor emeritus perhaps, film scholar perhaps, and the younger man in a casual shirt, jeans and running shoes, the assistant professor, lean, a little nervous. They moved away from the door now into partial darkness along the adjacent wall. He watched them a moment longer, the academics, adepts of film, of film theory, film syntax, film and myth, the dialectics of film, the metaphysics of film, as Janet Leigh began to undress for the blood-soaked shower to come.

When an actor moved a muscle, when eyes blinked, it was a revelation. Every action was broken into components so distinct from the entity that the watcher found himself isolated from every expectation.

Everybody was watching something. He was watching the two men, they were watching the screen, Anthony Perkins at his peephole was watching Janet Leigh undress.

Nobody was watching him. This was the ideal world as he might have drawn it in his mind. He had no idea what he looked like to others. He wasn't sure what he looked like to himself. He looked like what his mother saw when she looked at him. But his mother had passed on. This raised a question for advanced students. What was left of him for others to see?

For the first time he didn't mind not being alone here. These two men had strong reason to be here and he wondered if they were seeing what he was seeing. Even if they were, they would draw different conclusions, find references across a range of filmographies and disciplines. *Filmography*. The word used to make him draw back his head as if to put an antiseptic distance between him and it.

He thought he might want to time the shower scene. Then he thought this was the last thing he wanted to do. He knew it was a brief scene in the original movie, less than a minute, famously less, and he'd watched the prolonged scene here some days earlier, all broken motion, without suspense or dread or urgent pulsing screech-owl sound. Curtain rings, that's what he recalled most clearly, the rings on the shower curtain spinning on the rod when the curtain is torn loose, a moment lost at normal speed, four rings spinning slowly over the fallen figure of Janet Leigh, a stray poem above the hellish death, and then the bloody water curling and cresting at the shower drain, minute by minute, and eventually swirling down.

He was eager to watch again. He wanted to count the curtain rings, maybe four, possibly five or more or less. He knew that the two men at the adjacent wall would also be watching intently. He felt they shared something, we three, that's what he felt. It was the kind of rare fellowship that singular events engender, even if the others didn't know he was here.

Almost no one entered the room alone. They came in teams, in squads, shuffling in and milling briefly near the door and then leaving. One or two would turn and leave and then the others, forgetting what they'd seen in the seconds it took to turn and move toward the door. He thought of them as members of theater groups. Film, he thought, is solitary.

Janet Leigh in the long interval of her unawareness. He watched her begin to drop her robe. He understood for the first time that black-and-white was the only true medium for film as an idea, film in the mind. He almost knew why but not quite. The men standing nearby would know why. For this film, in this cold dark space, it was completely necessary, black-and-white, one more neutralizing element, a way in which the action becomes something near to elemental life, a thing receding into its drugged parts. Janet Leigh in the detailed process of not knowing what is about to happen to her.

Then they left, just like that, they were moving toward the door. He didn't know how to take this. He took it personally. The tall door slid open for the man with the cane and then the assistant. They walked out. What, bored? They went past the guard and were gone. They had to think in words. This was their problem. The action moved too slowly to accommodate their vocabulary of film. He didn't know if this made the slightest sense. They could not feel the heartbeat of images projected at this speed. Their vocabulary of film, he thought, could not be adapted to curtain rods and curtain rings and eyelets. What, plane to catch? They thought they were serious but weren't. And if you're not serious, you don't belong here.

Then he thought, Serious about what?

Someone walked to a certain point in the room and cast a shadow on the screen.

There was an element of forgetting involved in this experience. He wanted to forget the original movie or at least limit the memory to a distant reference, unintrusive. There was also the memory of this version, seen and reseen all week. Anthony Perkins as Norman Bates, a wading bird's neck, a bird's face in profile.

The film made him feel like someone watching a film. The meaning of this escaped him. He kept feeling things whose meaning escaped him. But this wasn't truly film, was it, in the strict sense. It was videotape. But it was also film. In the broader meaning he was watching a film, a movie, a more or less moving picture.

Her robe settling finally on the closed toilet lid.

The younger one wanted to stay, he thought, in scuffed running shoes. But he had to follow the traditional theorist with the braided hair or risk damaging his academic future.

Or the fall down the stairs, still a long way off, maybe hours yet before the private detective, Arbogast, goes backwards down the stairs, face badly slashed, eyes wide, arms windmilling, a scene he recalled from earlier in the week, or maybe only yesterday, impossible to sort out the days and viewings. Arbogast. The name deeply seeded in some obscure niche in the left brain. Norman Bates and Detective Arbogast. These were the names he remembered through the years that had passed since he'd seen the original movie. Arbogast on the stairs, falling forever.

Twenty-four hours. The museum closed at five-thirty most days. What he wanted was a situation in which the museum closed but the gallery did not. He wanted to see the film screened start to finish over twenty-four consecutive hours. No one allowed to enter once the screening begins.

This was history he was watching in a way, a movie known to people everywhere. He played with the idea that the gallery was like a preserved site, a dead poet's cottage or hushed tomb, a medieval chapel. Here it is, the Bates Motel. But people don't see this. They see fractured motion, film stills on the border of benumbed life. He understands what they see. They see one brain-dead room in six gleaming floors of crowded art. The original movie is what matters to them, a common experience to be relived on TV screens, at home, with dishes in the sink.

The fatigue he felt was in his legs, hours and days of standing, the weight of the body standing. Twenty-four hours. Who would survive, physically and otherwise? Would he be able to walk out into the street after an unbroken day and night of living in this radically altered plane of time? Standing in the dark, watching a screen. Watching now, the way the water dances in front of her face as she slides down the tiled wall reaching her hand to the shower curtain to secure a grip and halt the movement of her body toward its last breath.

A kind of shimmy in the way the water falls from the showerhead, an illusion of waver or sway.

Would he walk out into the street forgetting who he was and where he lived, after twenty-four hours straight? Or even under the current hours, if the run was extended and he kept coming, five, six, seven hours a day, week after week, would it be possible for him to live in the world? Did he want to? Where was it, the world?

He counted six rings. The rings spinning on the curtain rod when she pulls the curtain down with her. The knife, the silence, the spinning rings.

It takes close attention to see what is happening in front of you. It takes work, pious effort, to see what you are looking at. He was mesmerized by this, the depths that were possible in the slowing of motion, the things to see, the depths of things so easy to miss in the shallow habit of seeing.

People now and then casting shadows on the screen.

He began to think of one thing's relationship to another. This film had the same relationship to the original movie that the original movie had to real lived experience. This was the departure from the departure. The original movie was fiction, this was real.

Meaningless, he thought, but maybe not.

The day seeped away, with fewer people coming in, then nearly none. There was nowhere else he wanted to be, dark against this wall.

The way a room seems to slide on a track behind a character. The character is moving but it's the room that seems to move. He found deeper interest in a scene when there was only one character to look at, or, better maybe, none.

The empty staircase seen from above. Suspense is trying to build but the silence and stillness outlive it.

He began to understand, after all this time,

that he'd been standing here waiting for something. What was it? It was something outside conscious grasp until now. He'd been waiting for a woman to arrive, a woman alone, someone he might talk to, here at the wall, in whispers, sparingly of course, or later, somewhere, trading ideas and impressions, what they'd seen and how they felt about it. Wasn't that it? He was thinking a woman would enter who'd stay and watch for a time, finding her way to a place at the wall, an hour, half an hour, that was enough, half an hour, that was sufficient, a serious person, soft-spoken, wearing a pale summer dress.

Jerk.

It felt real, the pace was paradoxically real, bodies moving musically, barely moving, twelve-tone, things barely happening, cause and effect so drastically drawn apart that it seemed real to him, the way all the things in the physical world that we don't understand are said to be real.

The door slid open and there was a stir of mild traffic at the far end of the floor, people getting on the escalator, a clerk swiping credit cards, a clerk tossing items into large sleek museum bags. Light and sound, word-less monotone, an intimation of life-beyond, world-beyond, the strange bright fact that breathes and eats out there, the thing that's not the movies.

1

The true life is not reducible to words spoken or written, not by anyone, ever. The true life takes place when we're alone, thinking, feeling, lost in memory, dreamingly self-aware, the submicroscopic moments. He said this more than once, Elster did, in more than one way. His life happened, he said, when he sat staring at a blank wall, thinking about dinner.

An eight-hundred-page biography is nothing more than dead conjecture, he said.

I almost believed him when he said such things. He said we do this all the time, all of us, we become ourselves beneath the running thoughts and dim images, wondering idly when we'll die. This is how we live and think whether we know it or not. These are the unsorted thoughts we have looking out the train window, small dull smears of meditative panic.

The sun was burning down. This is what he wanted, to feel the deep heat beating into his body, feel the body itself, reclaim the body from what he called the nausea of News and Traffic.

This was desert, out beyond cities and scattered towns. He was here to eat, sleep and sweat, here to do nothing, sit and think. There was the house and then nothing but distances, not vistas or sweeping sightlines but only distances. He was here, he said, to stop talking. There was no one to talk to but me. He did this sparingly at first and never at sunset. These were not glorious retirement sunsets of stocks and bonds. To Elster sunset was human invention, our perceptual arrangement of light and space into elements of wonder. We looked and wondered. There was a trembling in the air as the unnamed colors and landforms took on definition, a clarity of outline and extent. Maybe it was the age difference between us that made me think he felt something else at last light, a persistent disquiet, uninvented. This would explain the silence.

The house was a sad hybrid. There was a corrugated metal roof above a clapboard exterior with an unfinished stonework path out front and a tacked-on deck jutting from one side. This is where we sat through his hushed hour, a torchlit sky, the closeness of hills barely visible at high white noon.

News and Traffic. Sports and Weather. These were his acid terms for the life he'd left behind, more than two years of living with the tight minds that made the war. It was all background noise, he said, waving a hand. He liked to wave a hand in dismissal. There were the risk assessments and policy papers, the interagency working groups. He was the out-sider, a scholar with an approval rating but no experience in government. He sat at a table in a secure conference room with the strategic planners and military analysts. He was there to conceptualize, his word, in quotes, to apply overarching ideas and principles to such matters as troop deployment and counter-insurgency. He was cleared to read classified cables and restricted transcripts, he said, and he listened to the chatter of the resident experts, the metaphysicians in the intelligence agencies, the fantasists in the Pentagon.

The third floor of the E ring at the Pentagon. Bulk and swagger, he said.

He'd exchanged all that for space and time. These were things he seemed to absorb through his pores. There were the distances that enfolded every feature of the landscape and there was the force of geologic time, out there somewhere, the string grids of excavators searching for weathered bone.

I keep seeing the words. Heat, space, stillness, distance. They've become visual states of mind. I'm not sure what that means. I keep seeing figures in isolation, I see past physical dimension into the feelings that these words engender, feelings that deepen over time. That's the other word, time.

I drove and looked. He stayed at the house, sitting on the creaky deck in a band of shade, reading. I hiked into palm washes and up unmarked trails, always water, carrying water everywhere, always a hat, wearing a broad-brimmed hat and a neckerchief, and I stood on promontories in punishing sun, stood and looked. The desert was outside my range, it was an alien being, it was science fiction, both saturating and remote, and I had to force myself to believe I was here.

He knew where he was, in his chair, alive to the protoworld, I thought, the seas and reefs of ten million years ago. He closed his eyes, silently divining the nature of later extinctions, grassy plains in picture books for children, a region swarming with happy camels and giant zebras, mastodons, sabertooth tigers.

Extinction was a current theme of his. The landscape inspired themes. Spaciousness and claustrophobia. This would become a theme.

Richard Elster was seventy-three, I was less than half his age. He'd invited me to join him here, old house, underfurnished, somewhere south of nowhere in the Sonoran Desert or maybe it was the Mojave Desert or another desert altogether. Not a long visit, he'd said.

Today was day ten.

I'd talked to him twice before, in New York, and he knew what I had in mind, his participation in a film I wanted to make about his time in government, in the blat and stammer of Iraq.

He would in fact be the only participant. His face, his words. This was all I needed.

First he said no. Then he said never. Finally he called and said we could discuss the matter but not in New York or in Washington. Too many goddamn echoes.

I flew to San Diego, rented a car and drove east into mountains that seemed to rise out of turns in the road, late summer thunderheads building, and then down through brown hills past rock-slide warnings and leaning clusters of spiny stalks and finally off the paved road and onto a primitive trail, lost for a time in the hazy scrawl of Elster's penciled map.

I arrived after dark.

"No plush armchair with warm lighting and books on a shelf in the background. Just a man and a wall," I told him. "The man stands there and relates the complete experience, everything that comes to mind, personalities, theories, details, feelings. You're the man. There's no offscreen voice asking questions. There's no interspersed combat footage or comments from others, on-camera or off."

"What else?"

"A simple head shot."

"What else?" he said.

"Any pauses, they're your pauses, I keep shooting."

"What else?"

"Camera with a hard drive. One continuous take."

"How long a take?"

"Depends on you. There's a Russian film, feature film, *Russian Ark*, Aleksandr Sokurov. A single extended shot, about a thousand actors and extras, three orchestras, history, fantasy, crowd scenes, ballroom scenes and then an hour into the movie a waiter drops a napkin, no cut, can't cut, camera flying down hallways and around corners. Ninety-nine minutes," I said.

"But that was a man named Aleksandr Sokurov. Your name is Jim Finley."

I would have laughed if he hadn't delivered the line with a smirk. Elster spoke Russian and he pronounced the director's name with an earthy flourish. This gave his remark an extra measure of self-satisfaction. I could have made the obvious point, that I wouldn't be shooting large numbers of people in textured motion. But I let the joke live out its full term. He was not a man who might make space for even the gentlest correction.

He sat on the deck, a tall man in wrinkled cotton trousers of landmark status. He went barechested much of the day, slathered with sunblock even in the shade, and his silvery hair, as always, was braided down into a short ponytail.

"Day ten," I told him.

In the morning he braved the sun. He needed to enrich his supply of vitamin D and raised his arms sunward, petitioning gods, he said, even if it meant the stealthy genesis of abnormal tissue.

"It's healthier to reject certain cautions than fall in line. I assume you know that," he said.

His face was long and florid, flesh drooping slightly at the sides of the jaw. He had a large pocked nose, eyes maybe grayish green, brows flaring. The braided hair should have seemed incongruous but didn't. It wasn't styled in sections but only woven into broad strands at the back of the head and it gave him a kind of cultural identity, a flair of distinction, the intellectual as tribal elder.

"Is this exile? Are you in exile here?"

"Wolfowitz went to the World Bank. That was exile," he said. "This is different, a spiritual retreat. The house used to be owned by someone in my first wife's family. I came here on and off for years. Came to write, to think. Elsewhere, everywhere, my day begins in conflict, every step I take on a city street is conflict, other people are conflict. Different here."

"But no writing this time."

"I've had offers to do a book. Portrait of the war room from the viewpoint of a privileged outsider. But I don't want to do a book, any kind of book."

"You want to sit here."

"The house is mine now and it's rotting

away but let it. Time slows down when I'm here. Time becomes blind. I feel the landscape more than see it. I never know what day it is. I never know if a minute has passed or an hour. I don't get old here."

"I wish I could say the same."

"You need an answer. Is that what you're saying?"

"I need an answer."

"You have a life back there."

"A life. That may be too strong a word."

He sat head back, eyes shut, face to the sun.

"You're not married, am I right?"

"Separated. We separated," I said.

"Separated. How familiar that sounds. Do you have a job, something you do between projects?"

Maybe he tried not to dose the word projects with fatal irony.

"Sporadic jobs. Production work, some editing."

He looked at me now. Possibly he was wondering who I was.

"Did I ask you once before how you got so scrawny? You eat. You throw down food same as I do."

"I seem to eat. I do eat. But all the energy, all the nourishment gets sucked up by the film," I told him. "The body gets nothing."

He closed his eyes again and I watched the sweat and sun lotion runneling slowly down his forehead. I waited for him to ask about filmwork I'd done on my own, the question I'd been hoping not to hear. But he'd lost interest in the conversation or simply had the kind of teeming ego that forgets to attend to such details. He would say yes or no based not on my qualifications but on the play of his mood, in his good time. I went inside to check my laptop for e-mail, needing outside contact but feeling corrupt, as if I were breaking an unstated pact of creative withdrawal.

He was reading poetry mostly, rereading his youth, he said, Zukofsky and Pound, sometimes aloud, and also Rilke in the original, whispering a line or two only, now and then, from the *Elegies*. He was working on his German.

I'd done one film only, an idea for a film, some people said. I did it, I finished it, people saw it but what did they see? An idea, they said, that remains an idea.

I didn't want to call it a documentary, although it was assembled completely from documents, old film footage, kinescopes of TV shows from the 1950s. This was social and historical material but edited well beyond the limits of information and objectivity and not itself a document. I found something religious in it, maybe I was the only one, religious, rapturous, a man transported.

The man was the one individual on-screen throughout, the comedian Jerry Lewis. This was Jerry Lewis of the early telethons, the TV shows broadcast once a year to benefit people suffering from muscular dystrophy, Jerry Lewis day and night and into the following day, heroic, tragicomic, surreal.

I looked at kinescopes of the early years, every distant minute, it was another civilization, midcentury America, the footage resembling some deviant technological lifeform struggling out of the irradiated dust of the atomic age. I edited out all the guest appearances, the lounge acts, movie stars, dancers, disabled children, the studio audience, the band. The film was all Jerry, pure performance, Jerry talking, singing, weeping, Jerry with his ruffled shirt open at the collar, bow tie undone, a raccoon flung over his shoulders, Jerry inviting the nation's love and wonder at four in the morning, in closeup, a crew-cut sweating man in semidelirium, a disease artist, begging us to send money to cure his afflicted children.

I had him babbling in unsequential edits, one year shading into another, or Jerry soundless, clowning, he is knock-kneed and bucktoothed, bouncing on a trampoline in slow motion, the old flawed footage, the disturbed signals, random noise on the soundtrack, streaky patterns on the screen. He inserts drumsticks in his nostrils, he sticks the handmike in his mouth. I added intervals of modern music to the track, rows of tones, the sound of a certain re-echoing drone. There was an element of austere drama in the music, it placed Jerry outside the moment, in some larger surround, ahistorical, a man on a mission from God.

I tormented myself over the running time, settling finally on a freakish fifty-seven-minute movie that was screened at a couple of documentary festivals. It could have been a hundred and fifty-seven minutes, could have been four hours, six hours. It wore me out, beat me down, I became Jerry's frenzied double, eyeballs popping out of my head. Sometimes a thing that's hard is hard because you're doing it wrong. This was not wrong. But I didn't want Elster to know about it. Because how would it make him feel, being a successor, a straight man to a rampaging comic.

My wife said to me once, "Film, film, film. If you were any more intense, you'd be a black hole. A singularity," she said. "No light escapes."

I said, "I have the wall, I know the wall, it's in a loft in Brooklyn, big messy industrial loft. I have access pretty much any time day or night. Wall is mostly pale gray, some cracks, some stains, but these are not distractions, they're not self-conscious design elements. The wall is right, I think about it, dream about it, I open my eyes and see it, I close my eyes it's there."

"You feel a deep need to do this thing. Tell me why," he said.

"You're the answer to that question. What you say, what you'll tell us about these last years, what you know that no one knows."

We were inside, it was late, he wore the old rumpled trousers, a cruddy sweatshirt, his big dumb feet in dressy leather sandals.

"I'll tell you this much. War creates a closed world and not only for those in combat but for the plotters, the strategists. Except their war is acronyms, projections, contingencies, methodologies."

He chanted the words, he intoned liturgically.

"They become paralyzed by the systems at their disposal. Their war is abstract. They think they're sending an army into a place on a map."

He was not one of the strategists, he said unnecessarily. I knew what he was, or what he was supposed to be, a defense intellectual, without the usual credentials, and when I used the term it made him tense his jaw with a proud longing for the early weeks and months,

35

before he began to understand that he was occupying an empty seat.

"There were times when no map existed to match the reality we were trying to create."

"What reality?"

"This is something we do with every eye-blink. Human perception is a saga of created reality. But we were devising entities beyond the agreed-upon limits of recognition or inter-pretation. Lying is necessary. The state has to lie. There is no lie in war or in preparation for war that can't be defended. We went beyond this. We tried to create new realities overnight, careful sets of words that resemble advertis-ing slogans in memorability and repeatability. These were words that would yield pictures eventually and then become three-dimen-sional. The reality stands, it walks, it squats. Except when it doesn't."

He didn't smoke but his voice had a sandlike texture, maybe just raspy with age, sometimes slipping inward, becoming nearly inaudible. We sat for some time. He was slouched in the middle of the sofa, looking off toward some point in a high corner of the room. He had scotch and water in a coffee mug secured to his midsection.

Finally he said, "Haiku."

I nodded thoughtfully, idiotically, a slow series of gestures meant to indicate that I understood completely.

"Haiku means nothing beyond what it is. A pond in summer, a leaf in the wind. It's human consciousness located in nature. It's the answer to everything in a set number of lines, a prescribed syllable count. I wanted a haiku war," he said. "I wanted a war in three lines. This was not a matter of force levels or logistics. What I wanted was a set of ideas linked to transient things. This is the soul of haiku. Bare everything to plain sight. See what's there. Things in war are transient. See what's there and then be prepared to watch it disappear."

"You used this word. Haiku," I said.

"I used this word. That's what I was there for, to give them words and meanings. Words they hadn't used, new ways of thinking and seeing. In one discussion or another, I probably used this word. They didn't fall out of their chairs."

I knew nothing about the men who didn't fall out of their chairs. But I was getting to know Elster and I wondered about the tactic, not that it mattered in the end. I wasn't interested in the impression he made on others, only in his feelings about the experience. Let him be wrong, rash, angry, weary. Lines and syllables. Old man's stale feet / fretful summer night. Et cetera.

"You wanted a war. Just a better one," I said.

"I still want a war. A great power has to act. We were struck hard. We need to retake the future. The force of will, the sheer visceral need. We can't let others shape our world, our minds. All they have are old dead despotic traditions. We have a living history and I thought I would be in the middle of it. But in those rooms, with those men, it was all priorities, statistics, evaluations, rationalizations."

The liturgical gloom was gone from his voice. He was tired and detached, too separated from events to do justice to his resentment. I made it a point not to provoke further comment. It would come when it mattered, self-generated, on-camera.

He finished his scotch but kept the mug nestled near his beltline. I was drinking vodka with orange juice and melted ice. The drink was at that stage in the life of a drink when you take the last bland sip and fade into rueful introspection, somewhere between self-pity and self-accusation.

We sat and thought.

I glanced over at him. I wanted to go to bed but didn't think I should leave before he did, not sure why, I'd left him there on other nights. It was dead still in the room, in the house, everywhere out there, windows open, nothing but night. Then I heard a mousetrap being triggered in the kitchen, hammer releasing, trap jumping.

There were three of us now. But Elster didn't seem to notice.

In New York he used a cane that he didn't need. He may have been feeling routine soreness in one knee but the cane was an emotional accessory, I was sure of this, adopted soon after his dismissal from the ministries of News and Traffic. He spoke vaguely of a knee replacement, talking more to himself than to me, making an argument for self-pity. Elster tended to be everywhere, in all four corners of a room, gathering impressions of himself. I liked the cane. It helped me see him, it lifted him from public print, a man who needed to live in a protective hollow, womblike and world-sized, free of the leveling tendencies of events and human connections.

In these desert days few things roused him from apparent calm. Our cars had four-wheel drive, this was essential, and after all his years here he seemed to be adjusting, still, to off-road driving, or any driving, anywhere. He asked me to program the GPS unit in his car. He wanted the system to be utilized, dared the system to work. He was grudgingly satisfied when it told him, in a spare male voice, what he already knew, *right turn in one point four miles*, leading him to the parking lot of the food market in town, twenty-five miles there, twenty-five back. He cooked for us every night, insisted on making dinner, showing no sign of the wariness people his age tend to feel about certain foods and how they affect the body that consumes them.

I took drives of my own looking for remote trailheads and then just sat in the car, conjuring the film, shooting the film, staring out at sandstone wastes. Or I drove into box canyons, over hard dry cracked earth, car swimming in heat, and I thought of my apartment, two small rooms, the rent, the bills, the unanswered calls, the wife no longer there, the separated wife, the crackhead janitor, the elderly woman who walked down the stairs backwards, slowly, eternally, four flights, backwards, and I never asked her why.

I talked to Elster about an essay he'd written a few years earlier, called "Renditions." It appeared in a scholarly journal and soon began to stir criticism from the left. This may have been his intention but all I could find in those pages was an implied challenge to figure out what the point was.

The first sentence was, "A government is a criminal enterprise."

The last sentence was, "In future years, of course, men and women, in cubicles, wearing headphones, will be listening to secret tapes

41

of the administration's crimes while others study electronic records on computer screens and still others look at salvaged videotapes of caged men being subjected to severe physical pain and finally others, still others, behind closed doors, ask pointed questions of flesh-and-blood individuals."

What lay between these sentences was a study of the word *rendition*, with references to Middle English, Old French, Vulgar Latin and other sources and origins. Early on, Elster cited one of the meanings of *rendering*—a coat of plaster applied to a masonry surface. From this he asked the reader to consider a walled enclosure in an unnamed country and a method of questioning, using what he called enhanced interrogation techniques, that was meant to induce a surrender (one of the meanings of *rendition*—a giving up or giving back) in the person being interrogated.

I didn't read the piece at the time, knew nothing about it. If I had known, before I knew Elster, what would I have thought? Word origins and covert prisons. Old French, Obsolete French and torture by proxy. The essay concentrated on the word itself, earliest known use, changes in form and meaning, zero-grade forms, reduplicated forms, suffixed forms. There were footnotes like nested snakes. But no specific mention of black sites, third-party states or international treaties and conventions.

He compared the evolution of a word to that of organic matter.

He pointed out that words were not necessary to one's experience of the true life.

Toward the end of the commentary he wrote about select current meanings of the word *rendition*—interpretation, translation, performance. Within those walls, somewhere, in seclusion, a drama is being enacted, old as human memory, he wrote, actors naked, chained, blindfolded, other actors with props of intimidation, the renderers, nameless and masked, dressed in black, and what ensues, he wrote, is a revenge play that reflects the mass will and interprets the shadowy need of an entire nation, ours.

I stood in a corner of the deck, out of the sun, and asked him about the essay. He waved it away, the entire subject. I asked him about the first and last sentences. They seem out of place in the larger context, I said, where crime and guilt don't get mentioned. The incongruity is pretty striking.

"Meant to be."

Meant to be. Okay. Meant to unsettle critics of the administration, I said, not the decision makers. Flat-out ironic.

He sat in an old reclining chair he'd found in the shed behind the house, a beach chair out of its element, and he opened one eye in lazy disdain, measuring the fool who states the obvious.

Okay. But what had he thought of the charge that he'd tried to find mystery and romance in a word that was being used as an instrument of state security, a word redesigned to be synthetic, concealing the shameful subject it embraced.

But I didn't ask this question. Instead I went inside and poured two glasses of ice water and came back out and sat in the chair alongside him. I wondered if he was right, that the country needed this, we needed it in our desperation, our dwindling, needed something, anything, whatever we could get, rendition, yes, and then invasion.

He held the cold glass to the side of his face and said he was not surprised by the negative response. The surprise came later, when he was contacted by a former university colleague and invited to a private meeting at a research institute just outside Washington. He sat in a paneled room with several others including the deputy director of a strategic assessment team that did not exist in any set of official records. He didn't mention the man's name, either because this was the kind of sensitive detail that must remain within the walls of a paneled room or because he knew that the name would mean nothing to me. They told Elster that they were seeking an individual of his interdisciplinary range, a man of reputation who might freshen the dialogue, broaden the viewpoint. His time in government would follow, interrupting a series of lectures he was giving in Zurich on what he called the dream of extinction, and after two years and part of another here he was, again, in the desert.

There were no mornings or afternoons. It was one seamless day, every day, until the sun began to arc and fade, mountains emerging from their silhouettes. This is when we sat and watched in silence.

At dinner later the silence held. I wanted to hear rain drumming down. We ate lamb chops that he'd grilled over charcoal on the deck. I ate head down, face in the plate. It was the kind of silent spell that's hard to break, becoming more dense with every bite we took. I thought about the dead time, the sense of self-entrapment, and I listened to us chew our food. I wanted to tell him how good it tasted but he'd cooked the chops too long, all traces of sweaty pink lost in flame. I wanted to hear wind in the hills, bats scratching in the eaves.

This was day twelve.

He looked at the beer glass in his hand and announced that his daughter would be coming to visit. It was like hearing that the earth had shifted on its axis, spinning night back into budding day. Significant news, someone else, a face and voice, called Jessie, he said, an exceptional mind, otherworldly.

I never asked the old woman what the reason was. I'd see her coming down the stairs backwards, clutching the handrail. I'd pause and watch, I'd offer to help, but never asked, never inquired into the problem, an injury, a matter of balance, a condition of mind. Just stood on the landing and watched her come down, step by step, a Latvian, this is all I knew, and New York City, this too, where people do not ask.

2

A great rain came sweeping off the mountains, too strong to think into, leaving us with nothing to say. We stood in the covered entrance to the deck, we three, watching and listening, world awash. Jessie held herself tightly, each flung hand clutching the opposite shoulder. The air was sharp and charged and when the rain stopped, in minutes, we went back to the living room and talked about what we were talking about when the sky broke open.

In those first days I thought of her as the Daughter. Elster's possessiveness, his enclosing space, made it hard for me to set her apart, to find some semblance of an independent being. He wanted her near him all the time.

When he said something meant for me, he always included her, drew her in through look or gesture. His eyes showed an eager glow that was not so rare, father regarding child, but it seemed to have the effect of smothering a response, or maybe she wasn't interested in making one.

She was pale and thin, mid-twenties, awkward, with a soft face, not fleshy but roundish and calm, and she seemed attentive to some interior presence. Her father said she heard words from inside them. I didn't ask what he meant by this. It was his job to say such things.

She wore jeans and sneakers, same as I did, and a loose shirt, and she was someone to talk to, which made the day pass. She said that she lived with her mother on the Upper East Side, an apartment she dismissed with a shrug. She did volunteer work with elderly people, shopping for food, taking them to their doctors. They had about five doctors each, she said, and she didn't mind sitting in the waiting room, she liked waiting rooms, she liked doormen hailing cabs, men in uniforms, it was the one uniformed thing you might see on an average day because cops were mainly hunched in cars.

I waited for her to ask where I lived, how I lived, with whom, whatever. Maybe it made her interesting, the failure to ask.

I said, "I had a studio out in Queens somewhere. I could afford it, then I couldn't. I work out of my apartment, which is more or less in Chinatown. I start projects, talk to people, think about other projects. Where will the money come from? I think about gap financing. I'm not sure what that means. I think about equity funding, foreign money, hedge funds. Every project becomes an obsession or what's the point. This is the one right now, your father. I know he's right for it and I have a feeling he knows it too. But I can't get an answer out of him. Do it, don't do it, maybe, never, some other time. I look at the sky and wonder. What the hell am I here for?"

"Company," she said. "The man totally physically hates to be alone."

"Hates to be alone but also comes here because there's nothing here, no one here. Other people are conflict, he says."

51

"Not the ones he chooses to be with him. A few students through the years, then there's lucky me, then my mother once upon a time. He has two sons from his first wife. Wrack and Ruin, he calls them. Don't even think of bringing up the subject of his sons."

Most of the time we talked about nothing, she and I. We had nothing in common, it seemed, but subjects kept flying by. She said she got confused when she stepped onto an escalator that wasn't functioning. This happened at the airport in San Diego, where her father was waiting to meet her. She stepped onto an up escalator that wasn't moving and she couldn't adjust to this, she had to self-consciously climb the steps and it was difficult because she kept expecting the steps to move and she'd sort of half walk but not seem to be going anywhere because the steps weren't moving.

She didn't drive a car because she couldn't do commands with her hands and feet. One of the people she helped care for had just died of multiple something-or-other. Her mother spoke Russian on the phone, blizzards of Russian day and night. She liked winter, snowfields in the park, but didn't go too far in, squirrels in winter might be rabid.

I liked these talks, they were quiet, with eerie depth in every stray remark she made. I stared at her sometimes, waiting for what, a return look, a show of discomfort. She had ordinary features, brown eyes, brown hair that she kept brushing back over her ear. There was something self-determined in her look, a blandness that seemed willed. It was a choice she'd made, to look like this, or so I told myself. Hers was another life, nowhere near mine, and it offered a release from the constant self-tunneling of my time here and also a kind of balance to her father's grip on my immediate future.

Elster in pajamas came dragging out of his bedroom to join us on the deck, barefoot, coffee mug in hand. He looked at Jessie and then smiled, seeming to remember in his grogginess that there was something he wanted to do. He wanted to smile.

He settled into a chair, speaking slowly, voice faint and scorched, bad night, early morning.

"Before I fell asleep, eventually, was thinking when I was a small kid how I'd try to imagine the end of the century and what a far-off wonder that was and I'd figure out how old I'd be when the century ended, years, months, days, and now look, incredible, we're here—we're six years in and I realize I'm the same skinny kid, my life shadowed by his presence, won't step on cracks on the sidewalk, not as a superstition but as a test, a discipline, still do it. What else? Bites the skin off the edge of his thumbnail, always the right thumb, still do it, loose piece of dead skin, that's how I know who I am."

I'd looked once in the medicine cabinet in his bathroom. Didn't have to open the cabinet door, there was no door. Ranks of bottles, tubes, pillboxes, nearly three shelves' worth, and a few other bottles, one uncapped, on the lid of the toilet tank, and several printed inserts scattered on a bench, unfolded, showing small bold cautionary typeface.

"Not my books, lectures, conversations, none of that. It's the goddamn hangnail, it's the dead skin, that's where I am, my life, there to here. I talk in my sleep, always did, my mother told me back then and I don't need anyone to tell me now, I know it, hear it, and this is more significant, somebody should make a study of what people say in their sleep and somebody probably has, some paralinguist, because it means more than a thousand personal letters a man writes in his lifetime and it's literature as well."

They weren't all prescription drugs but most were and all of it was Elster. The lotions, tablets, capsules, suppositories, the pastes and gels and the bottles and tubes they came in and the labels, inserts and price stickers—all this was Elster, vulnerable, and maybe there's supposed to be something morally degraded about my presence in the room but I didn't feel guilty, only intent on knowing the man and all those accessories of being, the mood-shifting agents, the habit-forming agents that no one sees or tries to imagine. Not that these things were serious aspects of the true life he liked to refer to, the lost thoughts, the memories that range through decades, the dead skin on the thumb. Still, in a way, here he was in his medicine cabinet, the man himself, marked out clearly in drops, tablespoons and milligrams.

"Look at all this," he said, not looking at it, the landscape and sky, which he'd indicated with a backwards sweep of the arm.

We didn't look at it either.

"Day turns to night eventually but it's a matter of light and darkness, it's not time passing, mortal time. There's none of the usual terror. It's different here, time is enormous, that's what I feel here, palpably. Time that precedes us and survives us."

I was becoming accustomed to this, his scale of address, long decades of thinking and speaking about transcendent matters. In this case he was speaking to Jessie, he'd been speaking to her all along, leaning forward in his chair.

She said, "The usual terror. What's the usual terror?"

"Doesn't happen here, the minute-to-minute reckoning, the thing I feel in cities."

It's all embedded, the hours and minutes, words and numbers everywhere, he said, train stations, bus routes, taxi meters, surveillance cameras. It's all about time, dimwit time, inferior time, people checking watches and other devices, other reminders. This is time draining out of our lives. Cities were built to measure time, to remove time from nature. There's an endless counting down, he said. When you strip away all the surfaces, when you see into it, what's left is terror. This is the thing that literature was meant to cure. The epic poem, the bedtime story.

"The film," I said.

He looked at me.

"Man at the wall."

"Yes," I said.

"Up against the wall."

"No, not as an enemy but a kind of vision, a ghost from the war councils, someone free to say whatever he wants, unsaid things, confidential things, appraise, condemn, ramble. Whatever you say, that's the film, you're the film, you talk, I shoot. No charts, maps, background information. Face and eyes, black-and-white, that's the film."

He said, "Up against the wall, motherfucker," and gave me a hard look. "Except the sixties are long gone and there are no more barricades."

"Film is the barricade," I told him. "The one we erect, you and I. The one where somebody stands and tells the truth."

"I never know what to say when he talks like that."

"He's been talking to students all his life," I said. "He doesn't expect anybody to say anything."

"Every second's the last breath he takes."

"Sits and thinks, that's what he's here for."

"And this movie you want to make."

"Can't do it alone."

"But isn't there a real movie you'd rather do? Because how many people will want to spend all that time looking at something so zombielike?"

"Right."

"Even if he ends up saying interesting things, it's something they could read in a magazine."

"Right," I said.

"Not that I go much to movies. I like old movies on television where a man lights a woman's cigarette. That's all they seemed to do in those old movies, the men and women. I'm normally so totally disregardless. But every time I see an old movie on television, I keep a sharp eye out for a man lighting a woman's cigarette."

I said, "Footsteps in movies."

"Footsteps."

"Footsteps in movies never sound real."

"They're footsteps in movies."

"You're saying why should they sound real."

"They're footsteps in movies," she said.

"I took your father to a movie once. Called *24 Hour Psycho*. Not a movie but a conceptual art piece. The old Hitchcock film projected so slowly it takes twenty-four hours to screen the whole thing."

"He told me."

"What did he tell you?"

"He told me it was like watching the universe die over a period of about seven billion years."

"We were there ten minutes."

"He said it was like the contraction of the universe."

"The man thinks on a cosmic scale. We know this."

"The heat death of the universe," she said.

"I thought he'd be interested. We were there and gone, ten minutes, he fled and I followed. Didn't talk to me all the way down six flights. He was using a cane then. Slow journey down, escalators, crowds, corridors, finally stairs. Not one word."

"I saw him that night and he told me. I thought I might want to see it. The whole point of nothing happening," she said. "The point of waiting just to be waiting. Next day I went."

"You stayed awhile?"

"I stayed awhile. Because even when something happens, you're waiting for it to happen."

"How long did you stay?"

"I don't know. Half an hour."

"That's good. Half an hour's good."

"Good, bad, whatever," she said.

Elster said, "When she was a child, she used to move her lips slightly, repeating inwardly what I was saying or what her mother was saying. She'd look very closely. I'd speak, she'd look, trying to anticipate my remarks word for word, nearly syllable for syllable. Her lips would move in nearest synchronization with mine."

Jessie was sitting across the table as he was speaking. We were eating omelettes, we ate omelettes nearly every night now. He was proud of his omelettes and tried to get her to watch as he broke the eggs, beat them with a fork and so on, talking all the way through the seasoning and olive oil and vegetables, enunciating the word *frittata*, but she wasn't interested.

"It was as though she was a foreigner learning English," he said. "She was right in my face, trying to define the words I was uttering, to absorb them and process them. She was looking, thinking, repeating, interpreting. Looking at my mouth, studying my lips, moving her lips. I have to tell you I was disappointed when she stopped doing this. Someone who truly listens."

He was looking at her, smiling.

"She talked to people then, strangers. Still does sometimes. You still do sometimes," he said. "Who do you talk to?"

Jessie shrugging.

"People on line at the post office," he said. "Nannies with children."

She chewed her food, head down, using the fork to twirl the omelette on the plate before she cut it.

We shared a bathroom, she and I, but she rarely seemed to be in there. A small airline kit, the only trace of her presence, was tucked into a corner of the windowsill. She kept soap and towels in her bedroom.

She was sylphlike, her element was air. She gave the impression that nothing about this place was different from any other, this south and west, latitude and longitude. She moved through places in a soft glide, feeling the same things everywhere, this is what there was, the space within.

Her bed was never made. I opened the bedroom door and looked several times but did not enter.

We sat out late, scotch for both of us, bottle on the deck and stars in clusters. Elster watched the sky, everything that came before, he said, there to see and map and think about.

I asked him whether he'd been to Iraq. He

needed to consider the question. I didn't want him to believe that I knew the answer and was asking the question in order to challenge the breadth of his experience. I didn't know the answer.

He said, "I hate violence. I fear the thought of it, won't watch violent movies, turn away from news reports on television that show dead or wounded people. I had a fight, I was a kid, I went into spasms," he said. "Violence freezes my blood."

He told me that he had all-source clearance, or access to every sensitive sliver of military intelligence. I knew this wasn't true. It was in his voice and face, a bitter wishfulness, and I understood of course that he was telling me things, true or not, only because I was here, we were both here, in isolation, drinking. I was his confidant by default, the young man entrusted with the details of his makeshift reality.

"I talked to them one day about war. Iraq is a whisper, I told them. These nuclear flirtations we've been having with this or that government. Little whispers," he said. "I'm telling you, this will change. Something's coming. But isn't this what we want? Isn't this the burden of consciousness? We're all played out. Matter wants to lose its self-consciousness. We're the mind and heart that matter has become. Time to close it all down. This is what drives us now."

He refilled his glass and passed me the bottle. I was enjoying this.

"We want to be the dead matter we used to be. We're the last billionth of a second in the evolution of matter. When I was a student I looked for radical ideas. Scientists, theologians, I read the work of mystics through the centuries, I was a hungry mind, a pure mind. I filled notebooks with my versions of world philosophy. Look at us today. We keep inventing folk tales of the end. Animal diseases spreading, transmittable cancers. What else?"

"The climate," I said.

"The climate."

"The asteroid," I said.

"The asteroid, the meteorite. What else?"

"Famine, worldwide."

"Famine," he said. "What else?"

"Give me a minute."

"Never mind. Because this isn't interesting to me. I have no use for this. We need to think beyond this."

I didn't want him to stop. We sat drinking quietly and I tried to think of further workable prospects for the end of human life on earth.

"I was a student. I ate lunch and studied. I studied the work of Teilhard de Chardin," he said. "He went to China, an outlaw priest, China, Mongolia, digging for bones. I ate lunch on open books. I didn't need a tray. The trays were stacked at the beginning of the line in the school cafeteria. He said that human thought is alive, it circulates. And the sphere of collective human thought, this is approaching the final term, the last flare. There was a North American camel. Where is it now?"

I nearly said, In Saudi Arabia. Instead I passed the bottle back to him.

"You told them things. Were these policy-board meetings? Who was there?" I said. "Cabinet-level people? Military people?"

"Whoever was there. That's who was there."

I liked this answer. It said everything. The

more I thought about it, the clearer everything seemed.

He said, "Matter. All the stages, subatomic level to atoms to inorganic molecules. We expand, we fly outward, that's the nature of life ever since the cell. The cell was a revolution. Think of it. Protozoa, plants, insects, what else?"

"I don't know."

"Vertebrates."

"Vertebrates," I said.

"And the eventual shapings. The slither, crawl, biped crouch, the conscious being, the self-conscious being. Brute matter becomes analytical human thought. Our beautiful complexity of mind."

He paused and drank and paused again.

"What are we?"

"I don't know."

"We're a crowd, a swarm. We think in groups, travel in armies. Armies carry the gene for self-destruction. One bomb is never enough. The blur of technology, this is where the oracles plot their wars. Because now comes the introversion. Father Teilhard knew this, the omega point. A leap out of our biology. Ask yourself this question. Do we have to be human forever? Consciousness is exhausted. Back now to inorganic matter. This is what we want. We want to be stones in a field."

I went in for ice. When I returned he was pissing off the deck, standing on tiptoe to get the emerging stream to clear the rail. Then we sat and listened to animal cries somewhere off in the thickets and we remembered where we were and didn't speak for a time after the sounds died away. He said he wished he had remained a student, gone to Mongolia, true remoteness, to live and work and think. He called me Jimmy.

"You'll have every opportunity to talk about these things," I said. "Talk, pause, think, talk. Your face," I said. "Who you are, what you believe. Other thinkers, writers, artists, nobody's done a film like this, nothing planned, nothing rehearsed, no elaborate setup, no conclusions in advance, this is completely sort of barefaced, uncut."

I spoke these lines in a whisky babble, half aware that I'd said all this before, and I heard a deep breath and then his voice, quiet and contained, even sad.

"What you want, my friend, whether you know it or not, is a public confession."

This could not be right. I told him absolutely not. I told him I had no intention of doing anything like that.

"A deathbed conversion. This is what you want. The foolishness, the vanity of the intellectual. The blind vanity, the worship of power. Forgive me, absolve me."

I fought off this notion, inwardly, and told him I had no special ideas beyond what I'd described.

"You want to film a man breaking down," he said. "I understand that. What's the point otherwise?"

A man melting into the war. A man who still believes in the righteousness of the war, his war. How would he look and sound on film, in a theater, on a screen anywhere, talking about a haiku war? Had I thought about this? I'd thought about the wall, the color and texture of the wall, and I'd thought about the man's face, the features that were strong but also collapsible in the show of whatever cruel truths might come spilling into his eyes, and then I thought about Jerry Lewis in closeup in 1952, Jerry ripping off his tie as he sang some weepy Broadway ballad.

Before he went inside Elster gripped my shoulder, reassuringly, it seemed, and I remained on the deck for some time, too deeply settled in my chair, in the night itself, to reach for the bottle of scotch. Behind me, his bedroom light went out, brightening the sky, and how queer it seemed, half the heavens coming nearer, all those incandescent masses increasing in number, the stars and constellations, because somebody turns off a light in a house in the desert, and I was sorry he wasn't here so I could listen to him talk about this, the near and far, what we think we're seeing when we're not.

I wondered if we were becoming a family, no more strange than most families except that we had nothing to do, nowhere to go, but that's not so strange either, father, daughter and whatever-I-was.

• • •

There was another thing she said, my wife, sympathetically, referring to the way I regarded life on the one hand and film on the other.

"Why is it so hard to be serious, so easy to be too serious?"

The bathroom door was open, midday, and Jessie was in there, barefoot, wearing a T-shirt and briefs, head over the basin, washing her face. I paused at the door. I wasn't sure whether I wanted her to see me there. I didn't imagine walking in and standing behind her and leaning into her, didn't see this clearly, my hands slipping under the T-shirt, my knees moving her legs apart so I could press more tightly, fit myself up and in, but it was there in some tenuous stroke of the moment, the idea of it, and when I moved away from the door I made no special effort to leave quietly.

The caretaker drove up, a squat man wearing a tractor cap and a stud in one ear. He looked after the house when Elster wasn't here, which was roughly ten months of the year, most years. I watched him go around to the side where the propane tank was located. When he came back this way I nodded as he went past me into the house. He showed no sign that he'd registered my presence. I thought he probably lived in one of the eccentric sprawls of shacks, trailers and cars on blocks, small crouched settlements sometimes visible from the paved roads.

Elster followed him into the kitchen speaking about a problem with the stove and I looked out toward the chalk hills and framed myself from that distance, clinically, man in landscape across the long day, barely seen.

Lunch was movable, flexible, eat when and where you want. I found myself at the table with Elster, who examined the processed cheese that Jessie had bought on our last trip to town. He said it was colored with spent uranium and then he ate it, slopped with mustard, between slices of prison bread, and so did I.

She was her father's dream thing. He didn't seem baffled by her stunted response to his love. It was natural for him not to notice. I'm not sure he understood the fact that she was not him.

When he finished the sandwich he moved forward in his chair, elbows on the table, voice lower now.

"I don't have to see a bighorn sheep before I die."

"Okay," I said.

"But I want Jessie to see one."

"Okay. We'll take a drive."

"We'll take a drive," he said.

"At some point we may have to get out of the car and climb. I think they spend time on rock ledges. I'd like to see one myself. I don't know why exactly."

He leaned in closer now.

"You know why she's here."

"I assume you wanted to see her."

"I always want to see her. Her mother, this was her mother's idea. There's a man Jessie sees."

"Okay."

"And her mother has certain ideas concerning his designs or just his general manner or his appearance or something. And she stated in her authoritarian way that possibly Jessie ought to put some distance between them, for now, temporarily, as a test of her attachment."

"So here she is. And you've talked to her about this."

"Tried to. She doesn't say much. There's no problem, that's what she says. Seems to like the guy. They see each other. They talk."

"How close are they?"

"They talk."

"Do they have sex?"

"They talk," he said.

We were both hunched over the table now, facing each other, speaking in uneasy whispers.

"Has she ever had an affair?"

"I admit I've wondered."

"No serious boyfriends."

"I don't think so, no, absolutely."

"Her mother sent her. This has to mean something."

"Her mother's a gorgeous woman, even today, but bad blood persists between us and when she sends the girl in my direction, yes, it means something. But she's also crazy. She's a completely manic individual who exaggerates everything."

"The guy's not a stalker. Nothing like that."

"Christ, no, not a stalker, I hate that word. Maybe persistent, that's all. Or stutters. Or has one brown eye and one blue eye."

"Wives. What a subject," I said.

"Wives, yes."

"How many?"

"How many. Two," he said.

"Just two. I thought maybe more."

"Just two," he said. "Feels like more."

"Both crazy. I'm only guessing."

"Both crazy. Over the years it ripens."

"What, being crazy?"

"You don't see it at first. Either they conceal it or it just needed to ripen. Once it does, it's unmistakable."

"But Jessie's the treasure, the blessing."

"That's right. And you?"

"No kids."

"Your wife. The separated wife. Is she crazy?"

"She thinks I'm crazy."

"You don't believe that," he said.

"I don't know."

"What are you protecting? She's crazy. Say it."

We were still whispering, we were bonding in whispers, but I wouldn't say it. I sat back and closed my eyes for a moment, seeing my apartment, clear and still and empty, four in the afternoon, local time, and there seemed more of me there in that dusty light than there was here, in the house or under open sky, but I wondered if I really wanted to go back to being the man who lives in the two rooms that are surrounded by the city that was built to measure time, in Elster's formulation, the slinking time of watches, calendars, minutes left to live.

Then I looked at him and asked if there was a pair of binoculars in the house. We'll need binoculars for the expedition, I said. He seemed puzzled by this. The bighorn sheep, I said. If we don't get swept away in a flash flood. If the heat doesn't kill us. We'll want to have binoculars handy to see detail. The male is the one with the horns, big and curved.

She said something funny at dinner about her eyes being closer together in New York, caused by serial congestion in the streets. Out here the eyes move apart, the eyes adapt to conditions, like wings or beaks.

Other times she seemed deadened to anything that might bring a response. Her look had an abridged quality, it wasn't reaching the wall or window. I found it disturbing to watch her, knowing that she didn't feel watched. Where was she? She wasn't lost in thought or memory, wasn't gauging the course of the next hour or minute. She was missing, fixed tightly within.

Her father tried hard not to notice these times. He sat across the room with his poets, moving his lips as he read.

I approached Richard Elster after a talk he gave at The New School and wasted no time, telling him about my idea for a film, simple and strong, I said, man and war, and he wasted no time either, leaving me rooted to a midsentence gesture but only momentarily. I followed him down the hall, speaking less rapidly, and then onto the elevator, still talking, and when we were out on the street he looked at me and commented on my appearance, saying that I looked like him when he was much younger, an underfed overworked student. I took this as encouragement, gave him my card and listened to him read it aloud, Jim Finley, Deadbeat Films. But he wasn't interested in being in a movie, mine or anyone's.

The second encounter was longer and stranger. Museum of Modern Art. No matter how many times I go to the museum, walking east to west, it's always farther down the street than it was last time. I was wandering through an exhibition on Dada and there was Elster, alone, stooped over a display case. I knew he'd written about the meanings of baby talk and so he'd clearly be interested in a major show of objects created in the name of demolished logic. I followed him for half an hour. I looked at the things he looked at. At times he leaned on his cane, other times simply carried it, haphazardly, horizontally, through tides of people. I told myself be calm, be civilized, speak slowly. When he moved toward the exit I approached him, reminded him of the earlier meeting, talked some baby talk and then urged him gently across the sixth floor to the gallery where the slow-winged *Psycho* was installed. We stood in the dark and watched.

I sensed nearly at once that Elster was resisting. Something was being subverted here, his traditional language of response. Stillborn images, collapsing time, an idea so open to theory and argument that it left him no clear context to dominate, just crisp rejection. Out on the street he spoke at last, mostly about his aching knee. No film, no chance, not ever.

A week later he telephoned and said he was in a place called Anza-Borrego, in California. I'd never heard of it. Then a hand-drawn map arrived in the mail, roads and jeep trails, and I caught a bargain flight the next afternoon. Two days, I thought. Three at most.

3

Every lost moment is the life. It's unknowable except to us, each of us inexpressibly, this man, that woman. Childhood is lost life reclaimed every second, he said. Two infants alone in a room, in dimmest light, twins, laughing. Thirty years later, one in Chicago, one in Hong Kong, they are the issue of that moment.

A moment, a thought, here and gone, each of us, on a street somewhere, and this is everything. I wondered what he meant by everything. It's what we call self, the true life, he said, the essential being. It's self in the soft wallow of what it knows, and what it knows is that it will not live forever.

• • •

I used to sit through the credits, all of them, when I went to the movies. It was a practice that worked against intuition and common sense. I was in my early twenties, unaffiliated in every respect, and I never left my seat until the full run of names and titles was completed. The titles were a language out of some ancient war. Clapper, armorer, boom operator, crowd costumes. I felt compelled to sit and read. There was a sense that I was capitulating to some moral failing. The starkest case of this occurred after the final shot of a major Hollywood production when the credits began to roll, a process that lasted five, ten, fifteen minutes and included hundreds of names, a thousand names. It was the decline and fall, a spectacle of excess nearly equal to the movie itself, but I didn't want it to end.

It was part of the experience, everything mattered, absorb it, endure it, stunt driving, set dressing, payroll accounting. I read the names, all of them, most of them, real people, who were they, why so many, names that haunted me in the dark. By the time the credits ended I was alone in the theater, maybe an old woman sitting somewhere, widowed, children never call. I stopped doing this when I began to work in the business, although I didn't think of it as a business. It was film, only that, and I was determined to do one, make one. *Un film. Ein film.*

Here, with them, I didn't miss movies. The landscape began to seem normal, distance was normal, heat was weather and weather was heat. I began to understand what Elster meant when he said that time is blind here. Beyond the local shrubs and cactus, only waves of space, occasional far thunder, the wait for rain, the gaze across the hills to a mountain range that was there yesterday, lost today in lifeless skies.

"Heat."

"That's right," Jessie said.

"Say the word."

"Heat."

"Feel it beating in."

"Heat," she said.

She was sitting in the sun, first time I'd seen her do this, wearing what she always wore, jeans rolled to the calves now, shirtsleeves to the elbows, and I stood in the shade watching.

81

"You'll die doing that."

"What?"

"Sitting in the sun."

"What else is there to do?"

"Stay inside and plan your day."

"Where are we anyway?" she said. "Do I even know?"

I wasn't using my cell phone and almost never touched my laptop. They began to seem feeble, whatever their speed and reach, devices overwhelmed by landscape. Jessie was trying to read science fiction but nothing she'd read so far could begin to match ordinary life on this planet, she said, for sheer unimaginableness. Her father found two handweights in a closet, seven or eight pounds each, made in Austria. How long have they been here? How did they get here? Who used them? He started using them now, lifting and breathing, lifting and gasping, one arm, then the other, up and down, sounding like a man in the midst of controlled strangulation, autoerotically asphyxiating.

What did I do? I filled the styrofoam cooler with bags of ice and bottles of water and took aimless drives, listening to tapes of blues singers. I wrote a letter to my wife and then tried to decide whether to send it or tear it up or wait a couple of days and then rewrite it and send it or tear it up. I tossed banana peels off the deck for animals to eat and I stopped counting the days since I'd arrived, somewhere around twenty-two.

In the kitchen he said, "I know about your marriage. You had the kind of marriage where you tell each other everything. You told her everything. I look at you and see this in your face. It's the worst thing you can do in a marriage. Tell her everything you feel, tell her everything you do. That's why she thinks you're crazy."

At dinner, over another omelette, he waved his fork and said, "You understand it's not a matter of strategy. I'm not talking about secrets or deceptions. I'm talking about being yourself. If you reveal everything, bare every feeling, ask for understanding, you lose something crucial to your sense of yourself. You need to know things the others don't know. It's what no one knows about you that allows you to know yourself."

• • •

Jessie rotated the glasses and dishes in the cabinet so we wouldn't use the same ones all the time and neglect the others. She did this in periodic spells of energy, a person possessed, working out a systematic arrangement in the sink, in the drain basket and on the shelves. Her father encouraged this. He dried the plates and then watched her shelve them, each in its determined slot. She was functioning, she was helping out around the house and she was doing it to an extreme degree, which was good, which was great, he said, because what's the meaning of doing dishes if you're not driven by something beyond sheer necessity.

He said to her, "Before you leave, I want you to see a bighorn sheep."

She went slack-jawed and held her hands out, palms up, like where did this come from, like what did I do to deserve this, eyes wide, a dumbfounded cartoon child.

The night she talked about art galleries in Chelsea.

She used to visit the galleries with a friend named Alicia. She said Alicia was deep as a dime. She said they'd walk down the long street choosing galleries at random and looking at the art and then walking down the street again and around the corner and up the next street, walking and looking, and one day she thought of something inexplicable. Let's do the same thing, up and down the same streets, but without going in the galleries. Alicia said *yes*, like instantly. They did this and it was quietly exciting, she said, it was like the idea of both their lifetimes. Walking down those long and mostly empty streets on weekday afternoons and unspokenly bypassing the art and then crossing the street and walking up the other side of the same street and turning the corner and going to the next street and walking down the next street and crossing to the other side and walking up the same street. Down and then up and then over to the next street, again and again, just walking and talking. It honestly deepened the experience, she said, made it better and more appreciative, street after street.

The night she stood on the edge of the deck, facing out into the dark, hands on the rail.

It was a nearly studied pose, unlike her, and I stood up, I wasn't sure why, just stood up, watching her. The light in Elster's bedroom was still on. I think I wanted her to turn and see me standing there. If I said something, she would know I was standing. The source of the voice would indicate I was standing and she would wonder why and then turn and look at me. This would tell me what she wanted, the way she turned, the look on her face, or what I wanted. Because I had to be smart, be careful. We were three of us alone here and I was the one in the middle, potential disrupter, the family fuckup.

When the light in Elster's bedroom went out I realized what an innocent reversion the moment was, teenage boy and girl from another era waiting for her parents to go to bed, except that her parents were divorced and bitter and her mother had gone to bed three hours ago, eastern standard time, and possibly not alone.

I asked her to come over and sit with me. I used that phrase, sit with me. She crossed the deck and we sat for a time. She said she'd been thinking about an elderly couple she took to doctors and helped at home sometimes. They all watched daytime TV and the woman kept looking at her husband to check his reaction to whatever the people on the screen were saying or doing. But he didn't have a reaction, he never had a reaction, he never even noticed that she was looking, and Jessie thought this was the whole long spectacle of a marriage sort of drop by drop, one head turning, the other head oblivious. They lost things all the time and spent hours and then days trying to find them, the mystery of disappearing objects, eyeglasses, fountain pens, tax documents, keys of course, shoes, one shoe, both shoes, and Jessie liked looking, she was good at it, all three of them moving through the apartment talking, looking, trying to reconstruct. The couple used old-fashioned fountain pens fed by actual ink. They were nice people, unfilthily rich, losing, misplacing, dropping all the time. They dropped spoons, dropped books, lost toothbrushes. They lost a painting, by a famous living American, that Jessie found at the back of a closet. Then she watched the wife look at

the husband to note his response and she realized that she'd become part of the ritual, one
watching the other watch the other.

They were as normal as people could be and
still be normal, she said. A little more normal,
they might be dangerous.

I reached over and took her hand, not sure
why. I liked thinking of her with those old
people, three innocents searching rooms for
hours. She let me do it, giving no sign that
she'd noticed. It was part of her asymmetry,
the limp hand, blank face, and it did not necessarily make me think the moment might
be extended to include other gestures, more
intimate. She was sitting next to anyone, talking through me to the woman in a sari on the
crosstown bus, to the receptionist in the doctor's office.

None of this mattered when her father's
light went on. I didn't know how to disengage
my hand without feeling ridiculous. The move
had to be strategic, not tactical, had to be full-
bodied, and I got up and walked over to the
rail, the hand an incidental detail. He came
out shuffling and moved past me, pajamas

smelling old, body old, the bedroom, the bed-
sheets, his dependable stink trailing the man
to his chair.

"Want a drink?"

"Scotch, neat," he said.

Inside I heard the screen door open and
shut and watched her cross the living room
and head down the hall, night over, one of a
hundred times I'd caught a glimpse of her or
moved past her or walked in the door as she was
walking out, a small lifetime of nonencounters,
like with your sister growing up, only carrying
static now, a random agitation in the air.

I took his scotch out to the deck, vodka for
me, one cube, vast night, moon in transit.
When she was a child, he said, and I waited
while he sipped his drink. She had to touch
her arm or face to know who she was. Happened rarely but happened, he said. She'd
put her hand to her face. This is Jessica. Her
body was not there until she touched it. She
doesn't remember this now, she was small, doctors, tests, her mother would pinch her, barest
response. She wasn't a child who needed imaginary friends. She was imaginary to herself.

We talked about nothing special then, household matters, a trip to town, but certain themes whispered at the margins. The father's love, that was one, and the other man's stalled life, and the young woman who didn't want to be here, and other questions as well, implicit, the war, his role, my film.

I said, "The camera's on a tripod. I sit alongside. You look at me, not at the camera. I use available light. Is there noise from the street? We don't care. This is primate filmmaking. The dawn of man."

A faint smile. He knew I was only talking. The reason for being here had begun to fade. I was simply here, only talking. I wanted to lose the notion of going back there, to responsibility, old woes, to the burn of beginning something that would lead nowhere. How many beginnings before you see the lies in your excitement? One day soon all our talk, his and mine, will be like hers, just talk, self-contained, unreferring. We'll be here the way flies and mice are here, localized, seeing and knowing nothing but whatever our scanted nature allows. A dim idyll in the summer flatlands.

"Time falling away. That's what I feel here," he said. "Time becoming slowly older. Enormously old. Not day by day. This is deep time, epochal time. Our lives receding into the long past. That's what's out there. The Pleistocene desert, the rule of extinction."

I thought of Jessie sleeping. She would close her eyes and disappear, this was one of her gifts, I thought, she drops into immediate sleep. Every night the same. She sleeps on her side, curled up, embryonic, barely breathing.

"Consciousness accumulates. It begins to reflect upon itself. Something about this feels almost mathematical to me. There's almost some law of mathematics or physics that we haven't quite hit upon, where the mind transcends all direction inward. The omega point," he said. "Whatever the intended meaning of this term, if it has a meaning, if it's not a case of language that's struggling toward some idea outside our experience."

"What idea?"

"What idea. Paroxysm. Either a sublime transformation of mind and soul or some worldly convulsion. We want it to happen."

"You think we want it to happen."

"We want it to happen. Some paroxysm."

He liked this word. We let it hang there.

"Think of it. We pass completely out of being. Stones. Unless stones have being. Unless there's some profoundly mystical shift that places being in a stone."

Our rooms had a common wall, hers and mine, and I imagined myself lying in bed, in shallow awareness, half hallucinatory, there's a word for this, and I tried to think of the word on two levels, seated on the deck and sprawled in bed, *hypnagogic*, that was it, and there is Jessie only a meter away, serenely dreaming.

"Enough for one night," he said. "Enough and enough."

He seemed to be looking for a place to put his glass. I took it from him and watched him go inside and soon his bedroom light went out.

Or wide awake, can't sleep, both of us, and she is lying on her back, legs apart, and I am sitting up and smoking although I haven't had a cigarette in five years, and she is wearing whatever she wears when she goes to bed, T-shirt to the thighs.

I was still holding Elster's glass. I put it on the deck and finished my drink, slowly, and set the glass down next to his. I went inside and turned off a couple of lights and then stood outside her room. There was space between door and jamb and I eased the door open and stood there, waiting for the dark to soften to the point where I could make out shapes. Then there she was, in bed, but it took some time before I realized she was looking at me. She was under the bedsheet looking straight at me and then she turned on her side and faced the far wall, pulling the sheet up to her neck.

Another moment passed before I drew the door quietly back to its original position. I went outside again and stood at the rail awhile. Then I adjusted the reclining chair to full length and lay flat on my back, eyes shut, hands on chest, and tried to feel like nobody nowhere, a shadow that's part of the night.

Elster drove in grim silence. This was routine. Even with no traffic, there were forces massed in opposition, depending on day and time— road conditions, threat of rain, impending nightfall, people in the car, the car itself. The GPS unit was okay, alerting him to turns, confirming the details of past experience. When Jessie was along, stretched across the rear seat, he'd try to listen to whatever she might be saying and the effort made him hunch toward the steering wheel in tense concentration. She liked to read road signs aloud, Restricted Area, Flash Flood Area, Call Box, Rock Slide Next 6 Miles. We were alone this time, he and I, going to town to stock up on groceries. He didn't want me to drive, he didn't trust other drivers, other drivers were not him.

In the market he moved along the shelves choosing items, tossing them in a basket. I did the same, we divided the store, moving quickly and capably and passing each other now and then in one of the aisles, avoiding eye contact.

On the way back I found myself engaged by the scribbled tar of repair work on the paved road. I was drowsy, staring straight ahead, and soon the spatter on the windshield seemed even more interesting than the tar. When we were off-road, on rubble, he reduced speed drastically and the easy bouncing nearly put me to sleep. My seat belt wasn't fastened. He usually said "Seat belts" when he started the car. I sat up straight and rolled my shoulders. I looked at the grit under my fingernails. The rule of seat belts was meant for Jessie but she didn't always comply. We went past a spindly creek bed and I wanted to pound the dashboard a few times, tom-tom-like, to get the blood pumping. But I just closed my eyes and sat there, nowhere, listening.

When we got back to the house she was gone.

From the kitchen he called her name. Then he went through the house looking. I wanted to tell him that she'd gone for a walk. But it would have sounded false. She didn't do that here. She hadn't done that since she'd arrived. I left the groceries on the kitchen counter and went outside to scan the immediate area, kicking through thorny bushes and ducking under mesquite snags. I wasn't sure what I was looking for. My rented car was where I'd left it. I checked the car's interior and then tried to detect fresh tire marks on the sandy approach to the house and later we both stood on the deck looking intently into the stillness.

It was hard to think clearly. The enormity of it, all that empty country. She kept appearing in some inner field of vision, indistinct, like something I'd forgotten to say or do.

We went into the house again and looked more closely, room to room, finding her suitcase, poking through her closet, opening drawers in the bureau. We hardly spoke, did not speculate on what or where. Elster spoke but not to me, a few puzzled mutterings about her unpredictability. I crossed the hall to the bathroom that she and I shared. Toilet kit on the windowsill. No note taped to the mirror. I threw back the shower curtain, making more noise than I'd intended.

Then I thought of the shed, how had we forgotten the shed. I felt a strange brainless elation. I told Elster. The shed.

This was the first time we'd gone anywhere without her. She hadn't wanted to come with us but we should have said something, and her father did, but we should have insisted, should have been unyielding.

All right it was not impossible, a long walk. The heat had diminished these past few days, there was cloud cover, even a breeze.

Maybe she didn't want to spend another minute here and walked all the way out to the nearest paved road hoping to hitch a ride. This was hard to believe, that she might expect to reach San Diego and then get on a flight to New York, apparently carrying nothing, not even a wallet. The wallet was on her dresser with bills and change scattered around it, credit card in its slot.

I stood at the entrance to the shed. A hundred years of junk, this is what I saw, glass, rags, metal, wood, alone here, we'd left her, and the feeling in the body, the sheer deadness in my arms and shoulders, and not knowing what to say to him, and the chance, the faint prospect that we'd be standing on the deck in faded light and she'd come walking along the sandpath and we'd barely believe what we were seeing, he and I, and it would take only moments to forget the past several hours and we'd go in to dinner and be the people we always were.

He was in the house, on the sofa, leaning well forward and talking into the floor.

"I tried to get her to come with me. I talked to her. You heard me. She said she wasn't feeling well. Headache. She gets headaches sometimes. She wanted to stay here and take a nap. I gave her an aspirin. I brought her an aspirin and a glass of water. I watched her swallow the damn thing."

He seemed to be trying to convince himself that all of this had happened precisely as he was stating it.

"We have to call."

"We have to call," he said. "But won't they say it's too early? She's only been gone an hour or two."

"They must get calls for lost hikers all the time. People missing all the time. Out here, this time of year, whatever the situation, they have to take action fast," I said.

The only phones were our cell phones, the quickest link we had to assistance of any kind. Elster had a map of the area with numbers he'd written down for the caretaker, the sheriff's office and the park rangers. I got both our phones and snatched the map off the kitchen wall.

I reached a man in the park rangers' office. I supplied name, description, rough location of Elster's house. I explained Jessie's circumstances, not a trailwalker or mountain biker, not driving a car, not prepared to withstand even a limited period in the elements. He said he was a volunteer and would try to reach the superintendent, who was with a search party now, looking for Mexicans who'd been led across the border and then abandoned, no food or water. There were search planes, tracking dogs, GPS hand units and they often searched at night. They would be on lookout, he said.

Elster was still on the sofa, phone at his side. No one answering in the sheriff's office, he'd left a message. He wanted to call the caretaker now, someone who knew the area, and I tried to recall the man clearly, face stained by sun and wind, eyes tight. If Jessie was the victim of a crime, I'd want to know where he was when it happened.

Elster called, phone rang a dozen times.

I finished putting away the groceries. I tried to concentrate on this, where things go, but objects seemed transparent, I could see through them, think through them. He was out on the deck again. I went through the house one more time, looking for an indication, a glimmer of intent. The impact, gathering from the first moment, hard to absorb. I didn't want to go out there and stand watch alongside him. The fear deepened in his presence, the foreboding. But after a while I poured scotch over ice in a tall glass and took it out to him and soon night was everywhere around us.

4

Passing into air, it seemed this is what she was meant to do, what she was made for, two full days, no word, no sign. Had she strayed past the edge of conjecture or were we willing to imagine what had happened? I tried not to think beyond geography, every moment defined by the desolation around us. But imagination was itself a natural force, unmanageable. Animals, I thought, and what they do to bodies in the wild, in the mind, no safe place.

The day before, with all the phone calls made and everyone alerted, I'd stood outside and seen a car on the horizon floating slowly into motion, rippled in dust and haze, as in a long shot in a film, a moment of slow expectation.

It was the local sheriff, broad red face, cropped beard. A helicopter was in the air, he said, trackers were on the ground. First thing he wanted to know was whether there had been any recent deviation in Jessie's normal pattern of behavior. The only deviation, I told him, was the fact that she was missing.

I walked him through the house. He seemed to be looking for signs of a struggle. He checked Jessie's room and spoke briefly to Elster, who sat on the sofa throughout, barely able to move, either from medication or lack of sleep. He said nearly nothing and showed confusion at the sight of a uniformed man in the house, large man shrinking the room, badge on his chest, gun at his belt.

Outside the sheriff told me that at this point there was no evidence of a crime to investigate. The procedure over time would be to coordinate a program with officials of other counties in order to examine motel records, phone records, car rentals, airline reservations and other matters.

I mentioned the caretaker. He said he'd

known the man for thirty years. The man was a volunteer naturalist, an expert on local plants and fossils. They were neighbors, he said, and then looked at me and listed a few categories of people in distress, ending with those who come to the desert to commit suicide.

Elster agreed to make the call, finally, the one to Jessie's mother. I tested locations for him and the clearest signal was outside, late afternoon, the man facing away from the house. He spoke Russian, his body sagged, it was hard for him to lift his voice above a whisper. There were long pauses. He listened, then spoke again, every word a plea, the response of an accused man, negligent, stupid, guilty. I stood nearby, understanding that his one lapse into awkward English was a helpless mimicry of hers, an expression of shared pain and parental identity. A helicopter appeared in the pale sky to the east and I watched him straighten his back, slowly, head raised, free hand blocking the sun.

Later I asked if he'd done what I'd told him to do. He looked away and walked toward his bedroom. I'd told him to raise the subject of Jessie's friend, the man she'd been seeing. Isn't this why her mother had sent her here? I stood at the door to his room. He sat on the bed, one hand raised in a gesture I could not interpret. What's the use or what's the connection or leave me alone.

He wanted pure mystery. Maybe it was easier for him, something beyond the damp reach of human motive. I was trying to think his thoughts. Mystery had its truth, all the deeper for being shapeless, an elusive meaning that might spare him whatever explicit details would otherwise come to mind.

But these weren't his thoughts. I didn't know what his thoughts were. I barely knew my own. I could think around the fact of her disappearance. But at the heart, in the moment itself, the physical crux of it, only a hole in the air.

I said, "Do you want me to call?"

"Doesn't make sense. Someone in New York."

"It's not supposed to make sense. What makes sense? Missing people never make sense," I said. "What's her name, Jessie's mother? I'll talk to her."

It wasn't until the following morning that he agreed to give me her phone number. Busy signal for half an hour, then an angry woman who resisted answering questions from someone she didn't know. The conversation went nowhere for a while. She'd met the man once, didn't know where he lived, how old he was exactly, what he did for a living.

"Just tell me his name. Can you do that?"

"She has three friends, girls, these names I know. Otherwise who she sees, where she goes, she doesn't listen to names, she doesn't tell me names."

"But this man. They went out together, yes. You met him, you said."

"Because I insisted. Two minutes he stands here. Then they leave."

"But he told you his name, or Jessie did."

"Maybe she told me, first name only."

She could not recall the name and this made her angrier. I put Elster on the phone and he said something to calm her. It didn't work but I wasn't giving up. I reminded her there was something about this man that she didn't like. Tell me, I said, and she responded ungrudgingly for a change.

For a week or longer there were phone calls. When she picked up, the caller put down the phone. She knew it was him, trying to reach Jessie. The ID screen displayed Blocked Caller. It was him every time, putting down the phone softly, and she could remember him standing in her doorway like someone you see three times a week, a delivery man with groceries, and you still don't know what he looks like.

"Last time I see Blocked Caller I pick up the phone and say nothing. Nobody is speaking. We are playing like it's a stupid game. I wait, he says nothing. He waits, I say nothing. Full minute. Then I say I know who you are. Man puts down the phone."

"You feel sure it was him."

"This is when I tell her she is going away."

"And once she went away."

"No more phone calls," the mother said.

He stopped shaving, I made it a point to shave every day, do nothing different. We waited for news. I wanted to get out, get in the car and join the searchers. But I imagined Elster with a mouthful of sleeping pills, the contents of a

106

bottle. I imagined a soggy lump, a glob, thirty or forty pills compacted and dripping spit. I sat and talked to him about the medications in his cabinet. Only the usual dose, I said. Double-check the directions, heed the warnings. I actually said this, heed the warnings, and the phrase did not seem stilted. I imagined him standing in the doorway of his bathroom, mouth forced partly open by the dense mass, a tentative attempt, a literal taste, one hand on each doorpost, bracing him.

Jessie had no cell phone but the police were checking records to see if she'd made or received calls on our phones. They were checking motel registers, reports of crimes in nearby counties and states.

"We can't leave."

"No, we can't."

"What if she comes back?"

"One of us has to be here," I said.

I was cooking the omelettes now. He seemed to wonder what he was supposed to do with the fork in his hand. I made coffee in the morning, set out bread, cereal, milk, butter and jam. Then I went to his bedroom and talked him out of bed. Nothing happened that was not marked by her absence. He ate sparingly. He moved through the house like someone mopping the floor, taking steps determined by laborious circumstance.

He was supposed to be in Berlin in a week, a lecture, a conference, he wasn't clear on the details.

He began to see things out of the corner of his eye, the right eye. He'd walk into a room and catch a glimpse of something, a color, a movement. When he turned his head, nothing. It happened once or twice a day. I told him it was physiological, same eye every time, routine sort of dysfunction, minor, happens to people of a certain age. He turned and looked. Someone there but then she wasn't.

I was counting the days again as I'd done in the beginning. Days missing. One of us was almost always on the deck, keeping watch. We did this well into the night. It became a ritual, a religious observance, and often, when both of us were out there, completely wordless.

We kept the door to her bedroom closed.

He began to resemble a recluse who might

live in a shack on an abandoned mining site, unwashed old man, shaky, stubbled, caution in his eyes, a fear from one step to the next that someone or something is waiting.

He referred to her now as Jessica, the real name, the birth name. He spoke in fragments, opening and closing his hand. I could watch him being driven insistently inward. The desert was clairvoyant, this is what he'd always believed, that the landscape unravels and reveals, it knows future as well as past. But now it made him feel enclosed and I understood this, hemmed in, pressed tight. We stood outside and felt the desert bearing in. Sterile thunder seemed to hang over the hills, stormlight washing toward us. A hundred childhoods, he said obscurely. Meaning what, the thunder maybe, a soft evocative rumble sounding down the years.

He asked me for the first time what had happened. Not what I thought or guessed or envisioned. What happened, Jimmy? I didn't know what to tell him. Nothing I might say to him was more or less likely than something else. It had happened, whatever it was, and there was no point thinking back into it, although we would of course, or I would. He had the intimate past to think back to, his and hers and her mother's. This is what he was left with, lost times and places, the true life, over and over.

A call late one night, the mother.

"I think I know his name."

"You think you know."

"I was sleeping. Then I wake up with his name. It is Dennis."

"You think it is Dennis."

"It is Dennis, for sure."

"First name Dennis."

"This is all I heard, first name. I wake up, just now, it is Dennis," she said.

At night the rooms were clocks. The stillness was nearly complete, bare walls, plank floors, time here and out there, on the high trails, every passing minute a function of our waiting. I was drinking, he was not. I wouldn't let him drink and he didn't seem to care. Sunsets were nothing more than dying light now, the dimming of chance. For weeks there had been nothing to do but talk. Now nothing to say.

The name sounded ominous, Jessica, sounded like formal surrender. I was the man who'd stood in the dark watching while she lay in bed. Whatever Elster's sense of implication, the nature of his guilt and failure, I shared it. He sat opening and closing his hand. When he heard helicopters beating down out of the sun, he looked up, surprised, always, then remembered why they were there.

We were often testing locations for cell phone reception, one of us facing one way, one of us the other, inside the house, outside, calling and getting calls, phone to one ear, free hand to the other, he is on the deck, I am forty yards down the path. I tried not to watch us when we did this. I wanted to stay within it, where the dance was a practical matter. I wanted to be free of seeing.

I began to use the old handweights he'd found earlier. I stood in my room lifting and counting. I called the park rangers and the sheriff. I could not forget what the sheriff had said. People come to the desert to commit suicide. I knew I had to ask Elster if she'd ever showed tendencies. Jessica. Was she seeing a doctor? Did she take antidepressants? Her airline kit was still in the bathroom we'd shared. I found nothing, talked to her father, called her mother, learned nothing from either that might indicate a drift in that direction.

I lifted the handweights one at a time, then both at once, twenty reps one way, ten the other, lifting and counting, on and on.

I led him out to the deck and put him in a chair. He was in pajamas and old tennis shoes, unlaced, his eyes seeming to trace a single thought. This is where he fixed his gaze now, not on objects but thoughts. I stood behind him with a pair of scissors and a comb and told him it was time for a haircut.

He turned his head slightly, in inquiry, but I repositioned it and began to trim his sideburns. I talked as I worked. I talked in a kind of audiostream, combing and cutting through the tangled strands on one side of his head. I told him this was different from shaving. The day would come when he'd want to shave and he'd have to do it himself but the hair on his head was a question of morale, his and mine. I said many empty things that morning, matter-of-factly, half believing. I removed the wormy rubberband from the weave of braided hair at the back of his neck and tried to comb and trim. I kept skipping to other parts of the head. He spoke about Jessie's mother, her face and eyes, his admiration, voice trailing off, low and hoarse. I felt compelled to trim the hair in his ears, long white fibers curling out of the dark. I tried to unsnarl every inch of matted vegetation before I cut. He spoke about his sons. You don't know this, he said. I have two sons from the first marriage. Their mother was a paleontologist. Then he said it again. Their mother was a paleontologist. He was remembering her, seeing her in the word. She loved this place and so did the boys. I did not, he said. But this changed over the years. He began to look forward to his time here, he said, and then the marriage broke up and the boys were young men and that was all he was able to say.

I stood to the side, head tilted, and studied my handiwork. I'd forgotten to drape a towel over his upper body and there were cuttings everywhere, hair on his face, neck, lap and shoulders, hair in his pajamas. I said nothing about the sons. I just kept cutting. If I had to give him a shower, I'd give him a shower. I'd stick his head in the kitchen sink and wash his hair. I'd scrub out the sour odor he carried with him. I told him I was almost done but I wasn't almost done. Then I realized there was something else I'd forgotten, some sort of brush to whisk away all this hair. But I didn't go inside to find one. I just kept cutting, combing out and cutting.

The call came early. Searchers had found a knife in a deep ravine not far from an expanse of land called the Impact Area, entry prohibited, a former bombing range littered with unexploded shells. They'd secured a perimeter around the object and were expanding the search. The ranger was careful not to refer to the knife as a weapon. Could be a hiker's or camper's, any number of uses. He set the approximate location of a dirt road that approached the site and when we finished talking I found Elster's map and quickly spotted the Impact Area, a large swatch of geometry with squared-off borders. There were thin wavery lines to the west—canyons, washes and mine roads.

Elster was in his room sleeping and I leaned over the bed and listened to him breathe. I don't know why I closed my eyes when I did this. Then I checked his medicine cabinet to make sure the number of pills and tablets in various bottles had not diminished by a notice-able amount. I made coffee, set a place for him and left a note saying I'd gone into town.

Blade seemed free of blood, the ranger had said.

I drove toward town and then veered east for a time and finally down toward the area in question. I left the paved road and followed a rutted track into a long sandy wash. Soon there were tall seamed cliff walls crowding the car and it wasn't long before I reached a vehicle dead end. I put on my hat, got out and felt the heat, the brunt, the force of it. I opened the trunk and raised the top of the cooler where a couple of water bottles lay in melted ice. I didn't know how far I was from the search site and tried to call the ranger but there was no signal. I moved around squat boulders dislodged from the heights by flash flooding or seismic events. The rough path here looked and felt like crumbled granite. Every so often I'd stop and look up and see a sky that seemed confined, compressed. I spent long moments looking. The sky was stretched taut between cliff edges, it was narrowed and lowered, that was the strange thing, the sky right there, scale the rocks and you can touch it. I started walking again and came to the end of the tight passage and into an open space choked at ground level with brush and stony debris and I half crawled to the top of a high rubble mound and there was the whole scorched world.

I looked out into blinding tides of light and sky and down toward the folded copper hills that I took to be the badlands, a series of pristine ridges rising from the desert floor in patterned alignment. Could someone be dead in there? I could not imagine this. It was too vast, it was not real, the symmetry of furrows and juts, it crushed me, the heartbreaking beauty of it, the indifference of it, and the longer I stood and looked the more certain I was that we would never have an answer.

I had to get out of the sun and skidded back down to flat land and a wedge of shade, where I took the water bottle out of my back pocket. I tried again to call the ranger. I wanted him to tell me where I was. I wanted to know where he was, with precise directions this time. I wanted to reach the scene just to see, to feel what was there. I assumed the knife was on its way to a crime lab somewhere in the county. I assumed the sheriff had acted on the information I'd given him about the phone calls that Jessie's mother had been getting from the Blocked Caller. Dennis. I thought of him as Dennis X. Was there legal cause to trace the phone calls? Did the mother remember the man's name correctly? Would the father still be in bed, swallowed by memories, immobilized, when I walked into the house? The water was lukewarm and chemical, broken down to molecules, and I drank some and poured the rest over my face and down my shirt.

I walked back into the wash under the shallow line of sky and then stopped and put my hand to the cliff wall and felt the tiered rock, horizontal cracks or shifts that made me think of huge upheavals. I closed my eyes and listened. The silence was complete. I'd never felt a stillness such as this, never such enveloping nothing. But such nothing that *was*, that spun around me, or she did, Jessie, warm to the touch. I don't know how long I stood there, every muscle in my body listening. Could I forget my name in this silence? I took my hand off the wall and put it to my face. I was sweating heavily and licked the moist stink off my fingers. I opened my eyes. I was still here, in the outside world. Then something made me turn my head and I had to tell myself in my astonishment what it was, a fly, buzzing near. I had to say the word to myself, *fly*. It had found me and come near, in all this streaming space, buzzing, and I swatted vaguely at the sound and then started back toward the dead end. I moved slowly and stayed near the wall, in intermittent shade. After a time I began to think I should have reached the car by now. I was tired, hungry, water was gone. I wondered whether this gap, this pass had a north and south fork and was it possible I had strayed into the wrong fork? I could not convince myself that it was not possible. The sky seemed to taper toward a point where the cliff walls met and I thought of turning back. I took the water bottle out of my pocket and tried to squeeze a drop or two into my mouth. Every few steps I told myself to turn back but kept going forward, increasing the pace. I wasn't sure that this was the same crushed granite path I'd come in on. I tried to recall color and texture, even the sound my shoes made on the coarse grains. Just when I knew I was lost I saw the trail widen slightly and then there was the car, a dusty shitpile of metal and glass, and I opened the door and fell into the seat. I put the key in the hole and hit the AC button and the fan button and a couple of other buttons. Then I sat back a moment and took a number of deep deliberate breaths. It was time to tell Elster we were going home.

That night I could not sleep. I fell into reveries one after another. The woman in the other room, on the other side of the wall, sometimes

Jessie, other times not clearly and simply her, and then Jessie and I in her room, in her bed, weaving through each other, turning and arching sort of sealike, wavelike, some impossible nightlong moment of transparent sex. Her eyes are closed, face unfrozen, she is Jessie at the same time that she is too expressive to be her. She seems to be drifting outside herself even when I bring her into me. I'm there and aroused but barely see myself as I stand at the open door watching us both.

I looked at him. The face was gradually sinking into the dense framework of the head. He was in the passenger seat and I said the words quietly.

"Seat belts."

He seemed to listen belatedly, knowing I'd spoken but failing to gather a meaning. He was beginning to resemble an x-ray, all eye sockets and teeth.

"Seat belts," I said again.

I buckled up and waited, watching him. We were taking the rented car, mine. I'd hosed down the car. I'd packed the bags and put them in the trunk. I'd made a dozen phone calls. He nodded this time and began to reach toward the strap over his right shoulder.

We were leaving her behind. This was hard to think about. We'd agreed at the beginning that one of us had to be here, always. Now an empty house into fall and through winter and no chance he'd ever return. I unbuckled my seat belt and leaned over to help him strap in. Then I drove into town to fill up the tank and soon we were out again moving through fault zones and between stands of swirled rock, the history that runs past the window, mountains forming, seas receding, Elster's history, time and wind, a shark's tooth marked on desert stone.

It was right to take him out of there. He'd be shivered down to a hundred pounds if we were to stay. I would take him to Galina, that was her name, the mother, and entrust the man to her compassion. Look at him, frail and beaten. Look at him, inconsolably human. They were together in this, I told myself. She would want to share the ordeal, I told myself. But I hadn't called her yet to say that we were heading home. Galina was the call I was afraid to make.

I kept glancing over. He sat back, eyes wide, and I talked to him the way I had when I was cutting his hair, rambling through that long morning, trying to keep him company, distract us both. But there was nearly no one to talk to now. He seemed beyond memory and its skein of regret, a man drawn down to sparest outline, weightless. I drove and talked, telling him about our flight, reporting our flight number, pointing out that we were wait-listed, reciting time of departure, time of arrival. Blank facts. In the sound of my words I thought I heard a flimsy strategy for returning him to the world.

The road began to climb, landscape going green around us, scattered houses, a trailer camp, a silo, and he started coughing and gasping, struggling to bring up phlegm. I thought he might choke. The road was tight and steep, guardrail at the edge, and there was nothing for me to do but keep going. He ejected the mess finally, hawked it up and spewed it into his open hand. Then he looked at it wobbling there and so did I, briefly, a thick stringy pulsing thing, pearly green. There was no place to put it. I managed to yank a handkerchief out of my pocket and toss it over. I didn't know what he saw in that handful of mucus but he kept looking.

We passed a row of live oaks. Then he croaked a few words.

"One of the ancient humors."

"What?"

"Phlegm."

"Phlegm," I said.

"One of the ancient and medieval humors."

The hanky sat on his thigh. I reached over and grabbed it, eyes on the road, and shook it out and placed it on his hand, over the blob. A helicopter passed somewhere behind us and I looked in the rearview mirror and then over at Elster. He didn't move, he sat with hand extended, draped in the cloth. Leaving her behind. We listened to the sound of the rotor dying away in the distance. He cleaned the mess from his hand and then crumpled the handkerchief and dropped it to the mat between his feet.

We drove in silence behind a motorboat being towed by a black pickup. I thought of his remarks about matter and being, those long nights on the deck, half smashed, he and I, transcendence, paroxysm, the end of human consciousness. It seemed so much dead echo now. Point omega. A million years away. The omega point has narrowed, here and now, to the point of a knife as it enters a body. All the man's grand themes funneled down to local grief, one body, out there somewhere, or not.

We passed through pinewoods and along a lake, small birds flying low to the water. His eyes were closed and his breathing a steady nasal hum. I tried to think about the future, unknown weeks and months ahead, and I realized what it was that had passed out of mind until this moment. It was the film. I remembered the film. Here it is again, man and wall, face and eyes, but not another talking head. On film the face is the soul. The man is a soul in distress, as in Dreyer or Bergman, a flawed character in a chamber drama, justifying his war and condemning the men who made it. It would never happen now, not a single frame. He would not have the firmness of will or the sheer heart for it and neither would I. The story was here, not in Iraq or in Washington, and we were leaving it behind and taking it with us, both.

The road began to descend toward the freeway now. He was belted in like a child, asleep. I thought about the airport, the luggage, getting him a wheelchair. I thought about the medieval humors. I kept looking at him, checking on him.

There we were, coming out of an empty sky. One man past knowing. The other knowing only that he would carry something with him from this day on, a stillness, a distance, and he saw himself in somebody's crowded loft, where he puts his hand to the rough surface of an old brick wall and then closes his eyes and listens.

Soon we were headed west, cars and trucks in clusters, rattling traffic, four lanes, and my cell phone rang. I paused a moment, then snatched it off my hip and said yes. No response. I said yes, glancing at the screen. BLOCKED CALLER. I said yes, hello, speaking louder. No response. I looked at Elster. His eyes were open now, head turned my way, more alert than I'd seen him in a week. I said yes and glanced at the screen.

BLOCKED CALLER. I hit the off switch and slid the phone into the case clipped to my belt.

I hated freeway driving, traffic heavier now, cars shooting across lanes. I kept my eyes on the road. I didn't want to look at him, didn't want to hear any questions or speculations. I was thinking six things at once. The mother. She remembered his name in her sleep. I was thinking someone's returning my call. That's all it was, all it could be, someone I knew returning my call of last evening or earlier this morning, friend, colleague, landlord, weak signal, failed transmission. What did it mean? It meant that soon the city would be happening, nonstop New York, faces, languages, construction scaffolds everywhere, the stream of taxis at four in the afternoon, off-duty signs lighted.

I thought of my apartment, how distant it would seem even when I walked in the door. My life at a glance, everything there, music, movies, books, the bed and desk, the seared enamel around the burners on the stove. I thought of the telephone ringing as I entered.

Anonymity 2

September 4

Norman Bates, scary bland, is putting down
the phone.

The man stood at the wall thinking ahead.
He'd started doing this, jumping scenes,
speeding through scenes mentally, visually,
with closing time not too far off. He didn't
want to check his watch. He tried to contain
his impatience, to direct every energy toward
the screen, see what is happening now.

The door easing everlastingly open.

The strip of interior light spreading across
the floor as the door continues to move.

The shadow of the door vanishing under
the door.

These abstract moments, all form and scale,

the carpet pattern, the grain of the floorboards, binding him to total alertness, eye and mind, and then the overhead shot of the landing and the attack on Arbogast.

His visits to the gallery mingled seamlessly in memory. He could not recall on which day he'd watched a particular scene or how many times he'd watched certain scenes. Could they be called scenes, becalmed as they were, the raw makings of a gesture, the long arc of hand to face?

He was in place, as always, his place, in body contact with the north wall. People in uneasy passage, in and out. They would stay longer, he thought, if there were chairs or benches here. But any kind of seating arrangement would sabotage the concept. The bare setting, and the darkness, and the chill air, and the guard motionless at the door. The guard purified the occasion, made it finer and rarer. But what was he guarding? The silence maybe. Or the screen itself. They might climb the screen and claw it, tourists from the movie malls.

Standing was part of the art, the standing man participates. That was him, sixth straight day he'd been here, last day of the installation. He would miss being in this room, free at times to walk around the screen and to observe from the reverse side, to note the left-handedness of people and objects. But always back to the wall, in physical touch, or he might find himself doing what, he wasn't sure, transmigrating, passing from this body into a quivering image on the screen.

The dull parts of the original movie were not dull anymore. They were like everything else, outside all categories, open to entry. This is what he wanted to believe. But he yielded to the screen more readily at certain times. He conceded this, the screen empty of characters, the screen that reveals a stuffed bird or a single human eye.

Three children entered, two boys and a girl, interchangeably blond, with a woman behind them.

He could not understand why the detective, Arbogast, clearly stabbed once below the heart, goes hurtling down the stairs with stab wounds on his face. Maybe the viewer is expected to imagine a second and third and fourth knife slash but he wasn't willing to do this. There was a clear discrepancy between the action and the visible effect.

He tried to consider the complexities of editing. He tried to think in terms of the conventional projection. He couldn't recall spotting the problem when he'd last seen the movie, on TV. Maybe the error is not detectable at twenty-four frames per second. He'd read somewhere that this is the speed at which we perceive reality, at which the brain processes images. Alter the format and expose the flaws. This was a flaw that a person might tend to excuse unless he was a man of attenuated viewpoint. If that was him, then that was him.

The children lingered just inside the door, not sure whether they wanted to investigate whatever it was they'd walked into, and the woman slipped along the side wall and paused and looked at the screen and then moved to the juncture of the two walls. He watched the kids gradually withdraw their attention from the film and glance around them. Where are they, what is this? One of them looked toward the door, where the guard stood, staring into the daylong narrows of his detachment.

Arbogast is still falling down the stairs.

He thought again of a situation. The children made him think of this, a situation in which the film is shown beginning to end over twenty-four consecutive hours. Hadn't this happened somewhere, once, different museum, different city? He considered how he might set the terms of such a showing. Select audience. No children, no casual viewers. Entry forbidden once the screening begins. What if someone wants to leave, has to leave? All right you can leave. Leave if you absolutely have to. But once out, you do not re-enter. Make it a personal test of endurance and forbearance, a kind of punishment.

But punishment for what? Punishment for watching? Punishment for standing here day after day, hour after hour, in hapless anonymity? He thought of others. That's what others might say. But who were these others?

The woman seemed to slide along the wall invisibly, in little fixed increments. He could barely see her and was certain she could not see him. Was she with the children or not?

The children were three bright objects, ages maybe eight to ten, gathering light from the screen, where lurid death was being scratched out in microseconds.

Anthony Perkins as Norman Bates. Norman Bates as Mother, crouched at the foot of the stairs now, in a widow's wig and floor-length dress. He gathers himself spiderlike over the detective, who is supine on the hall carpet, and resumes the business of stabbing.

Anonymous, he and the museum guard. Was the guard who was here today the same guard of the previous five days? Was the guard of the previous five days the same guard all day long? They must switch guards at some point during the day but he had failed to notice or had forgotten. A man and woman entered, parents of the kids, genetic code crackling in the air. They were large people in khaki shorts, tremendously three-dimensional, with tote bags and knapsacks. He watched the film, looked at others, watched the film. Through it all, the mind working, the brain processing. He didn't want this day to end.

Then somebody said something.

Somebody said, "What am I looking at?"

It was the woman to his left, standing closer now, and she was speaking to him. He was confused by this. The question made him stare harder at the screen. He tried to absorb what she'd said. He tried to deal with the fact that someone was standing next to him. This hadn't happened before, not here. And he tried to adjust to the other thing that hadn't happened, that was sort of never supposed to happen. Being spoken to. This woman standing somehow next to him was changing every rule of separation.

He looked at the screen, trying to consider what he might say. He had a good vocabulary except when he was talking to someone.

Finally he whispered, "The private detective. Man on his back."

It was a constricted whisper and he wasn't sure she'd heard him. But the response was nearly immediate.

"Do I want to know who's stabbing him?"

Again he had to think a moment before he decided on an answer. He decided on the answer no.

He said this, "No," shaking his head to indicate finality, if only to himself.

He waited for some time, watching hand and knife in midframe, isolated, and again it came, the voice nowhere near a whisper.

"I want to die after a long traditional illness. What about you?"

The interesting thing about this experience, until now, was that it was all his. No one knew he was here. He was alone and unacknowledged. There was nothing to share, nothing to take from others, nothing to give to others.

Now this. Out of nowhere, walks into the gallery, stands next to him at the wall, talks to him in the dark.

He was taller than she was. At least there was that. He wasn't looking at her but knew he was taller, somewhat, slightly. Didn't have to look. He sensed it, felt it.

The blond children went moping after their parents and out the door and he imagined them leaving black-and-white behind forever. He watched Janet Leigh's sister and Janet Leigh's lover talking in the dark. He didn't regret the loss of dialogue. He didn't

134

want to hear it, didn't need it. He would not be able to watch the real movie, the other *Psycho*, ever again. This was the real movie. He was seeing everything here for the first time. So much happening within a given second, after six days, twelve days, a hundred and twelve, seen for the first time.

She said, "What would it be like, living in slow motion?"

If we were living in slow motion, the movie would be just another movie. But he didn't say this.

Instead he said, "I guess this is your first time."

She said, "Everything's my first time."

He waited for her to ask him how many times he'd been here. He was still adjusting to the presence of another person but isn't this what he'd wanted these past days, a movie companion, a woman, someone willing to discuss the film, evaluate the experience?

She told him she was standing a million miles outside the fact of whatever's happening on the screen. She liked that. She told him she liked the idea of slowness in general. So many things go so fast, she said. We need time to lose interest in things.

Either the others could not hear them or did not care. He looked straight ahead. He was certain that the museum would close before the movie reached its actual end, its story end, Anthony Perkins wrapped in a blanket, the eyes of Norman Bates, the face coming closer, the sick smile, the long implicating look, the complicit look at the person out there in the dark, watching.

He was still waiting for her to ask him how many times he'd been here.

Day after day, he'd say. Lost count.

What's your favorite scene, she'd say.

I take it moment by moment, second by second.

He couldn't think of what she might say next. He thought he'd like to leave for a minute, go to the men's room and look in the mirror. Hair, face, shirt, same shirt all week, just look at himself briefly and then wash his hands and hurry back. He worked out the location in advance, men's room, sixth floor, he needed to see himself in the event she stayed until closing time and they left the gallery together and stood in the light. What would she be seeing when she looked at him? But he remained where he was, eyes on the screen.

She said, "Where are we, geographically?"

"The movie starts in Phoenix, Arizona."

He wasn't sure why he'd named both city and state. Was the state necessary? Was he talking to someone who didn't necessarily know that Phoenix is in Arizona?

"Then the locale changes. California, I think. There are road signs and license plates," he said.

A French couple came in. They were French or Italian, intelligent-looking, standing in the faint light near the sliding door. Maybe he'd said Phoenix, Arizona, because the words appeared on the screen after the opening credits. He tried to remember if the name of Janet Leigh's character was part of the opening credits. Janet Leigh as—but the name hadn't registered if he'd seen it at all.

He was waiting for the woman to say something. He remembered in high school when being shorter than the girl he was talking to made him want to fall on the floor and get kicked by passersby.

"Some movies are too visual for their own good."

"I don't think this one," he said. "I think this one is worked out carefully, shot for shot."

He thought about this. He thought about the shower scene. He thought about watching the shower scene with her. That might be interesting, together. But because it had been shown the day before, and because each day's screening was discontinued when the museum closed, the shower scene would not be part of today's viewing. And the curtain rings. Was he completely sure there are six rings spinning on the curtain rod when Janet Leigh in her dying fall pulls the shower curtain down with her? He wanted to watch the scene again, to reaffirm the curtain rings. He'd counted six, he was sure of six, but he needed to reaffirm.

Such second thoughts go on and on and the situation intensified the process, being here, watching and thinking for hours, standing and watching, thinking into the film, into himself. Or was the film thinking into him, spilling through him like some kind of runaway brain fluid?

"Have you been looking at other things in the museum?"

"Came straight here," she said, and that's all she said, disappointingly.

He could tell her things about the story and characters but maybe that could wait for later, with luck. He thought of asking what she did. Like two people learning a language. What do you do? I don't know, what do you do? This was not the kind of conversation they ought to be having here.

He wanted to think of them as two like souls. He imagined them staring at each other for a long moment, here in the dark, a frank and open look, a truthful look, strong and probing, and then they stop staring and turn and watch the film, without a word passing between them.

Janet Leigh's sister is coming toward the camera. She is running into darkness, a beautiful thing to see, decelerated, the woman running, shedding background light as she comes, face and shoulders faintly shaped, total dark falling in around her. This is what they ought to talk about here, if they talk, when they talk, light and shadow, the image on the screen, the room they're in, talk about where they are, not what they do.

He tried to believe that the tension in his body alerted her to the drama of the scene. She would sense it, next to him. This is what he thought. Then he thought about combing his hair. He wasn't carrying a comb. He would have to smooth down his hair with his hands once he got in front of a mirror, wherever and whenever, unnoticeably, or some reflecting surface on a door or pillar.

The French couple changed position, moving across the room to the west wall. They were a positive presence, attentive, and he was sure they would talk about the experience for hours afterward. He imagined the cadence of their voices, the pattern of stress and pause, talking through dinner in a restaurant recommended by friends, an Indian place, a Vietnamese place, Brooklyn, remote, the harder to get to, the better the food. They were outside him, people with lives, it was a question of actuality. This woman, the one next to him, as he regarded her, was a shadow unfolding from the wall.

"You're sure this isn't a comedy?" she said. "I mean, just looking at it."

She was watching the tall spooky house looming over the low motel, the turreted house where Mother sometimes sits by the bedroom window and where Norman Bates assumes the vesture of cross-dressing hell.

He thought about this, about Norman Bates and Mother.

He said, "Can you imagine yourself living another life?"

"That's too easy. Ask me something else."

But he couldn't think of something else to ask. He wanted to dismiss the idea that the film might be a comedy. Was she seeing something he had missed? Did the slow pulse of projection reveal something to one person and conceal it from another? They watched the sister and the lover talk to the sheriff and the wife. He wondered if he could work the conversation around to dinner, although there was no conversation right now.

Maybe we could get a bite nearby, he would say.

I don't know, she'd say. I might have to be somewhere in half an hour.

He imagined turning and pinning her to the wall with the room emptied out except for the guard who is looking straight ahead, nowhere, motionless, the film still running, the woman pinned, also motionless, watching the film over his shoulder. Museum guards should wear sidearms, he thought. There is priceless art to protect and a man with a gun would clarify the act of seeing for the benefit of everyone in the room.

"Okay," she said, "gotta go now."

He said, "You're leaving."

It was a flat statement, you're leaving, spoken reflexively, stripped of disappointment. He hadn't had time to feel disappointed. He checked his watch for no reason. It was something to do rather than stand there dumbly. In theory it gave him time to think. She was already moving toward the door and he hurried after her, but quietly, eyes averted from anyone who might be watching. The door slid open and he was behind her, out into the light and onto the escalator, floor to floor, and then across the lobby and through the revolving door to the street.

He caught up to her, careful not to smile or touch, and said, "What about doing this sometime at a real movie with seats to sit on and people on the screen who laugh and cry and shout?"

She paused to listen, half turning toward him, middle of the sidewalk, bodies pushing past.

She said, "Would that be an improvement?"

"Probably not," he said, and this time he smiled. Then he said, "Do you want to know something about me?"

She shrugged.

"I used to multiply numbers in my head when I was a kid. A six-digit number times a five-digit number. Eight digits times seven digits, day and night. I was a pseudo genius."

She said, "I used to read what people were saying on their lips. I watched their lips and knew what they were saying before they said it. I didn't listen, I just looked. That was the thing. I could block out the sound of their voices as they said what they were saying."

"As a kid."

"As a kid," she said.

He looked directly at her.

"If you'll give me your phone number, I could call you sometime."

She shrugged okay. That was the meaning of the shrug, okay, sure, maybe. Although if she saw him on the street an hour from now, she probably wouldn't know who he was or where she'd met him. She recited the number quickly and then turned and walked east into the midtown glut.

He went into the crowded lobby and found a cramped space on one of the benches. He put his head down to think, to duck away from it all, the sustained pitch of voices, languages, accents, people in motion carrying noise with them, lifetimes of noise, a clamor bouncing off the walls and ceiling and it was loud and surrounding, making him cower down. But he had her phone number, this is what mattered, the number was securely in mind. Call her when, two days, three days. In the meantime sit and think about what they'd said, what she looked like, where she might live, how she might spend her time.

That's when the question came to mind. Did he ask her name? He didn't ask her name. He made the inner gesture of reproving himself, a finger-wagging cartoon of teacher and child. Okay, this is another matter he would be able to think about. Think about names. Write down names. See if you can guess the name from the face. The face had brightened slightly when he talked about the numbers he did in his head as a kid. Not brightened but sort of loosened, her eyes showing interest. But the story wasn't true. He did not multiply large numbers in his head, ever. This was something he said sometimes because he thought it would help explain him to others.

He sneaked a look at his watch and did not hesitate, crossing to the ticket area and paying full price. Should be half adult, considering the hour, or free, should be free. He blinked at the ticket in his hand and hurried to the sixth floor, two steps at a time on the escalator, everybody going the other way. He entered the dark gallery. He wanted to bathe in the tempo, in the near static rhythm of the image. The French couple was gone. There was one person and the guard and then him, here for the last less-than-an-hour. He found his place at the wall. He wanted complete immersion, whatever that means. Then he realized what it means. He wanted the film to move even more slowly, requiring deeper involvement of eye and mind, always that, the thing he sees tunneling into the blood, into dense sensation, sharing consciousness with him.

Norman Bates, scary bland, is putting down the phone. He will turn off the light in the motel office. He will move along the stepped path to the old house, several rooms lighted, dark sky beyond. Then a series of camera shots, varying angles, he remembers the sequence, he stands at the wall and anticipates. Real time is meaningless. The phrase is meaningless. There's no such thing. On the screen Norman Bates is putting down the phone. The rest has not happened yet. He sees in advance, afraid that the museum will close before the scene ends. The announcement will sound throughout the museum in all the languages of the major museum nations and Anthony Perkins as Norman Bates will still be going up the stairs to the bedroom, where Mother is lying long dead.

The other person walks out the tall door. There is only him and the guard now. He imagines all motion stopping on the screen, the image beginning to shudder and fade. He imagines the guard removing the sidearm from his holster and shooting himself in the head. Then the screening ends, the museum closes down, he is alone in the dark room with the body of the guard.

He is not responsible for these thoughts. But they're his thoughts, aren't they? He returns his attention to the screen, where everything is so intensely what it is. He watches what is happening and wants it to happen more slowly, yes, but he is also mind-racing ahead to the moment when Norman Bates will carry Mother down the stairs in her white bedgown.

It makes him think of his own mother, how could it not, before she passed on, two of them contained in a small flat being consumed by rising towers, and here is the shadow of Norman Bates as he stands outside the door of the old house, the shadow seen from inside, and then the door begins to open.

The man separates himself from the wall and waits to be assimilated, pore by pore, to dissolve into the figure of Norman Bates, who will come into the house and walk up the stairs in subliminal time, two frames per second, and then turn toward the door of Mother's room.

Sometimes he sits by her bed and says something and then looks at her and waits for an answer.

Sometimes he just looks at her.

Sometimes a wind comes before the rain and sends birds sailing past the window, spirit birds that ride the night, stranger than dreams.

ACKNOWLEDGMENT

24 Hour Psycho, a videowork by Douglas Gordon, was first screened in 1993 in Glasgow and Berlin. It was installed at the Museum of Modern Art in New York in the summer of 2006.

picador.com

blog
videos
interviews
extracts